CL1/19

CU00596995

*West*ern

Leeds Library and Information Service
24 hour renewals
http://www.leeds.gov.uk/librarycatalogue
or phone 0845 1207271
Overdue charges may apply

LD 5060234 9

Return to Crows Creek

Return to Crows Creek is the second in the series following the adventures of Englishman Marshal Daniel Wheetman, who has been given over to President Hayes by Queen Victoria in an attempt to bring justice to the lawless west. However, Daniel's methods of policing are in complete contrast to those employed by other US sheriffs and marshals; he cannot ride a horse, does not believe in the use of firearms and has a personality that makes the vast majority of cowboys want to blow his head off – but together with his rough, tough deputies, Murphy Patterson and Moses Carver, they travel to Cactus Ridge to solve the problem of the murder of a young woman who had been a leading figure in the temperance movement.

By the same author

Crows Creek

Return to Crows Creek

John E. Vale

A Black Horse Western

ROBERT HALE

© John E. Vale 2018
First published in Great Britain 2018

ISBN 978-0-7198-2866-9

The Crowood Press
The Stable Block
Crowood Lane
Ramsbury
Marlborough
Wiltshire SN8 2HR

www.bhwesterns.com

Robert Hale is an imprint
of The Crowood Press

Typeset by
Derek Doyle & Associates, Shaw Heath
Printed and bound in Great Britain by
4Bind Ltd, Stevenage, SG1 2XT

CHAPTER 1

Murphy's eyes opened slowly as he began to wake up to a head splitting, nerve shattering, almighty and unearthly sound. His nostrils filled with the smothering smell of smoke and brimstone and the intense heat was almost overpowering as he shook the unconscious body of his fellow deputy.

'Carver,' he whispered. 'Carver, wake up. . . I think we've done died and gone straight to hell.'

Carver moaned, turned over, went back to sleep and rattled as he snored.

In sheer frustration Murphy began to kick Carver's legs. 'No, this is it!' he insisted. 'I'm telling yer, we've died and gone straight to hell.'

'What?' Carver gasped as he sprang bolt upright in disbelief. 'You mean Old Nick has come and taken our souls?'

Murphy looked at the flying embers as they rose high into the air and gulped. 'I reckon so. The thing is, Carver, I done some stuff I maybe ought not to have done, but I was always told I could ask and

5

would be forgiven. Amen.'

Carver reached for his pistol. 'Hey, I ain't got my iron.'

'Shhh!' Murphy whispered. 'I ain't got mine neither because if'n when you die you have to leave all earthly chattels behind,' he explained solemnly.

'So why've I still got me boots and such?'

'That's not for me to say, but the point is we're unarmed and it's best not rile him none because he's master of the underworld . . . I was told all about him by preacher Father O'Donnell. That was when I was knee high to a grasshopper and used to go to Sunday school.'

'The hell you say? You went to Sunday school?'

'I do say, and if we had got guns it wouldn't do no good fixin' to blast our way outta here, because what we need to do is beg for our souls to be spared.'

'The hell you say?' Carver replied as he began to mull matters over. 'Hey, Murphy, what do ya reckon we died of?'

Murphy rubbed his chin and shook his head. 'I ain't sure, but maybe we fell out of a tree.'

'A tree? Why in the name of hell would we have fallen from a tree?'

'Because I once fell out of a tree when I was ten, tryin' to look into Tyler Oldburn's sister's bedroom. I landed in a pile of horse shit and I ached somethin' crazy, like I do now.'

'We both couldn't have felled from no tree, not both at the same time, and I ain't never heard of what's his name's sister.'

'Well *you* explain why we hurt so bad and I smell of horse shit.'

Together they stopped whispering as an unearthly rhythmic pumping got louder and louder. The leaping shadows and intense heat told them the flames were getting higher, and a deathly scream echoed in their ears. 'I can hear him breathin' fire and torment to some other poor soul.' Carver said nervously.

Murphy crawled to the balcony's edge, slowly stood up and carefully peered over, fully expecting to see the Devil stoking up the fires of hell when all he saw was the rotund shape of Henry Copeland, the ever cheery blacksmith.

'Afternoon, boys,' Henry shouted. 'I was wonderin' when you two would wake up.'

'Henry, is that you?' Carver shouted in disbelief.

'Who else would you goddamned expect to be here?' Henry replied.

Murphy gave a sigh of relief. 'How in the name of blazes did we get here?'

Henry put down his hammer, doused a metal bar in cold water, scratched his head and sat down on his anvil. 'Don't either of you two remember anything?'

'Remember what?' Murphy asked.

Henry shook his head in disbelief. 'Remember what the pair of you got up to last night?'

'Such as?'

'"Such as?" Between the pair of you, you wrecked half the town, not to mention those you toyed with!'

Carver popped up next to Murphy and gave a

childish grin. 'The hell you say?'

'Hey, Henry, how did we get to be up here?' Murphy asked. 'I ain't seen no staircase.'

'A few of the drovers from the Eagle Mountain Ranch carried you both from the Star Diamond, hauled you up there on ropes and took away the ladder. The marshal told 'em to do it, sayin' as to how this'll keep you out of trouble. With the both of you not bein' able to get down an' all, he figured the town would be safe.'

'Why ain't he locked us up in jail?' Murphy asked.

'Jail's full. What with all those prisoners you took, there ain't no more room.'

Carver sniffed and cleared his system with an almighty three-second belch. 'If'n what you say is true then where's our guns?' he asked.

'You gave them to the marshal just after you both started cheatin' at cards.'

'I ain't never cheated at cards!' Murphy insisted.

'Oh, I beg to differ,' Henry told them sternly. 'I was watchin', so was the marshal, and he was writin' in that little book of his too.'

Murphy narrowed his eyes. 'Just how was I cheatin'?'

'Well, after your arrestin' the Bannisters, some of the townsfolk were mighty grateful and bought you both a drink or two.' He blew on his fingernails and polished them on his leather apron as his face lit up with pride. 'As a matter of fact they bought me one or two as well. . . . Me helping you boys out an' all that. Anyways, you two were both drunker than Old

Stumpy when you started cheatin' one another. As I remember it, Murphy, you came up with five aces, and then you, Carver, you came up with six kings. The whole hotel was in an uproar laughin' and so was you two, so you played on to see as to who could cheat the best; that's when the marshal got your guns.'

'He took our guns?'

'No, as I said, you *gave* the marshal your guns.'

Carver began to laugh. 'Now I know you's a-joshin'; we'd never give up our guns.'

'Maybe not ordinarily but the marshal bet you both five dollars you wouldn't give him your guns and you did it just to win the bet.'

Carver grinned and shook his head. 'And you say Marshal Wheetman is supposed to be smart . . . He done lost ten dollars, that ain't so smart. Haw haw!'

'Anyroads,' Henry continued. 'As I was telling yer, the both of you thought it a good idea to have a duel. Seein' as you had no guns you decided to settle the whole thing in a shin kickin' contest.' He slapped his thigh and rolled with laughter. 'I swear, Murphy, you was a riot. You got a long red feather from Alice's fruit hat and stuck it in your neck collar, then went about struttin' and crowin' like a twenty dollar rooster, flappin' your arms and scratchin' your feet until it came to the contest. Carver, you went first and kicked Murphy so hard I almost limped for ya.

'Murphy, you went around hoppin' in a circle and cursin' so bad, Old Jack Hargrove went on to blushin'. Then it came to your turn, Murphy, but you

9

was so drunk you missed Carver and hit the table leg. Might have broken your own had the table leg not come adrift and flew straight through Alice's best coloured window. She was hoppin' mad and comenst to hittin' you both with a switch that she kept behind the bar. The pair of you ran like naughty little children and headed for the street whilst Alice kept on switchin' you both real good.'

'Outside you both fell about laughin' so hard, I swear I thought you'd never breathe in agen.'

'And that's how we got to be up in your loft?' Murphy asked.

'Oh no, that's just the start. Next you went to the Golden Shoe and got even more liquored up. By this time there was quite an audience and Ben Crookshank bet you both five dollars you couldn't stay on Gloria, his mule, for more'n a minute. You both thought it was a duel so you took the bet.'

'Murphy . . . the way you jumped on backwards and held on to its tail was a sight for sore eyes; you even used your teeth, but it bucked you off in seconds and you landed like a rag doll in a pile of horse shit.'

'Carver, you jumped on all cocky like and held tighter than a snake with a gopher with your arms wrapped around Gloria's neck. At first she looked surprised and stood stone still, and maybe you'd have lasted longer had you not sat bolt upright a-wavin' your arms high in the air like some big galoot. Gloria turned her head and looked at you pitifully before throwing you back into the Golden Shoe, straight through the front window. Jack Lang was so riled up he told you never to step into his saloon agen.'

Murphy rubbed his aching back. 'And that's how we ended up here?'

''Fraid not, boys, only the beginnin'. You see, the duel hadn't come to no outcome so you both decided to continue with the contest.'

'But you said as to how we were carried from the Golden Shoe, and just then you said as how Jack Lang told us never to return.'

'That's true, boys, but you did return . . . and return you did in big style.'

'All the folks thought you'd gone to sleep off all that liquor, but that weren't the case. Before too long the pair of you came ridin' down the street on the backs of two giant hogs. You were shoutin', screamin' and hollerin' so loud the whole darned mob of Ted Hanley's pigs were in tow . . . I tell yer, boys, it was an even bigger sight for sore eyes.'

'You, Murphy . . . you began to get ahead a little, so Carver done grabbed your hog's tail and tried to slow it down. It began a screamin' and cussin' and blow me if'n it didn't head straight towards the Golden Shoe followed by Carver's hog and all the rest of Ted's stock.'

'Did I win?' Murphy asked.

'Not entirely, because your hog went straight under the saloon doors and you were sittin' high on its back, sort of turning a little as you were hand flappin' your hat to loosen Carver's grip on your hog . . . and that's when it happened.'

11

'What happened?'

'You were swept off like fresh snow from a newly polished saddle.'

'So I won?' Carver asked.

''Fraid not, either. Murphy grabbed you and sent you a-flyin' to the floor.'

'So then what happened next?' Murphy asked.

'The rest of the hogs followed your two and ran about inside the Golden Shoe. Well, I guess they must have been pretty scared because they did what nature intended as they ran here and there, causin' a right ruckus. Boys, I swear Jack Lang will never get rid of the smell. Neither will his worship Nathaniel Boyd. Funny thing is, he was wearin' a brand new pair of pigskin boots when he done slipped and fell into the biggest pile of hog shit I have ever clapped my eyes on.'

'Dan Tripmaster began pointing and a-laughin' at his worship, so Mrs Boyd done hit Dan with her ladies parasol – the one she claims come from Paris, France. Dan fell back and turned over a table at which were sittin' two cowhands I ain't never seen afore. One of 'em pushed Dan and Dan pushed him back, and soon a fight began to break out. Tables, chairs, bottles and glasses were being threwd. I swear I ain't never seen anythin' like it afore.'

Murphy closed his eyes, shook his head and sighed. 'And the marshal? Where was he?'

'The marshal sat halfway up the stairs, writin' in that little book of his. He didn't seem at all bothered. I reckon he knew it would all simmer down sometime so he just watched and wrote.'

'And then?' Murphy asked.

'Well, that's just it, boys, it's as I told ya. Just before you both passed out you were hauled up there and left to sober up.'

'The marshal told 'em to do it, you say?'

'Sure did,' Henry grinned. 'I reckon you's both in a heap of trouble. Maybe it'll be safer to stay put until the whole thing blows over.'

'When do ya think that'll be?'

'Oh, next fall I reckon.'

Looking like an old scarecrow after a tornado, Carver moved his shattered body and staggered to the edge of the loft. 'Henry, put that ladder into place. We're goin' to come on down.' After Henry did as he was asked, Carver descended to the ground slowly, with a groan. 'Oh, my achin' back. I think one of those hogs must have run me down,' he complained.

'Not rightly true,' Henry continued. 'As the drovers were draggin' you over here, Olga was as angry as a bull on a red flag day and blamed you for Murphy being drunk an' all. Said as to how "it vaz all ze fault of dirty Carver and how she should have killed him when she had zee chance".'

'Olga!' Carver gasped in fear.

Henry nodded his head. 'Olga,' he replied knowingly. 'She took to grapplin' those drovers and thumpin' you hard so as they would let you go and she could then commence to stomp on your head. As it was, the marshal said something to her in that

13

fancy lingo of hers and she plumb cooled down.'

Murphy came down the ladder and strained as her tried to straighten up. 'I bet the marshal is pretty angry?'

'You could say that, but not as mad as many of the townsfolk: those hogs you released went on to eatin' Roy Weston's vegetable patch. They done damn near ate the lot before they could be stopped, Mary Brinkster and her sister lost two lines of clean washin' and they ate all of Gary Stalker's apple store.'

Murphy scratched his head. 'That ain't rightfully our fault,' he protested. 'Ted Hanley should keep his hogs fed. Why, if'n it hadn't been for us, those hogs could have starved to death.'

'I don't think Ted thinks of it that way, but if he was struggling to feed 'em all, his job's a little easier now because four on 'em got shot. If I were you boys, I would stay low for a while.'

'It still ain't our fault: we were drunk,' Murphy insisted. 'We don't know nothin' of any hog race, although I do seem to recollect hittin' the saloon doors.'

Henry glanced across the street and saw the marshal making his way towards the smithy. 'You boys had better hide,' he told them. 'The marshal is headed this way.'

Murphy and Carver rushed to the back of the smithy and covered themselves with some tarpaulins. 'Good afternoon, Mister Copeland. I take it my deputies are awake?' Daniel asked.

'Awake and gone, Marshal,' Henry replied with a

smile. 'I reckon they must feel mighty rough after last night. Maybe they took off out of town?'

Daniel thought for a moment then surveyed the interior of the smithy slowly. 'Dust, Mister Copeland.'

'Errr . . . I'm sure I don't know what you mean, Marshal.'

'Dust, as in "earth to earth, ashes to ashes, dust to dust". You notice dust comes last, after ashes. That is true in your establishment, Mister Copeland, as it is true in all blacksmiths all over the world: dust comes last.' He began to saunter towards the tarpaulins as he removed his sword from his stick. 'The dust is quite thick over here; one could almost cut the atmosphere with a knife, or a sword in this case.' He gave the blade a quick swish through the air. 'Did you hear that, Mister Copeland, the sound of a razor sharp blade, menacingly cutting its way as one wields it with a smooth sharp slash? They say many a head has been severed with a good deep slash but *that* method of dispatching one's adversary is a trifle vulgar, don't you think?' He gently felt the needle sharp point of his sword. 'I much prefer to thrust rather than slash.' He stabbed his sword elegantly through the top right hand side of one tarpaulin. 'See how easily it could penetrate the human chest.'

'Easy, Marshal,' Henry said. 'I need those without holes if'n you please.'

Daniel stood and paused in front of the tarpaulins under which Murphy and Carver were hiding and assumed his finest *en garde* position.

'It's over, boys!' Henry shouted. 'Best come out

now; the marshal's got you figured.'

Slowly, the top of the tarpaulins began to peel away, revealing the ashen faces of Murphy and Carver. 'Errr. . . Howdy, Marshal,' Murphy began. 'Me and Carver here were both tryin' to sober up before we came on to see ya.'

'That's right,' Carver added. 'We thought it ain't right, us comin' to see yer all hungover and such, and Henry has told us what we did last night and . . . well, for my part, I'm plumb sorry.'

'That goes for me too, Marshal, and if'n there's a way to make amends I reckon we'll find it.' He put his hand on his heart. 'That's if you'll give us the chance, that is.'

Just as they were trying to win over the marshal, a large dark shape appeared at the door, blocking out much of the light. 'I come for to give you a baaath,' Olga said menacingly.

Murphy and Carver stood bolt upright in fear. 'Now wait a minute, Olga, that ain't hardly right,' Murphy insisted. 'I done had a bath last week and I've got some clean duds in my room; all I needs is a quick rinse and I'll be good as new.'

Olga's eyes peered at Carver as she pointed. 'I vont him for me to give a bath too.'

'Carver!' Murphy gasped. 'But that ain't hardly right either . . . I mean he's only just arrived in town, and neither of you have had no chance to get acquainted. Besides, he ain't the one who fell in horse shit.'

As Olga moved towards Carver he held out his

16

right hand in protest, only to have it grasped, pulled, hoisted and used to throw the rest of his helpless body over Olga's shoulder. 'I take him now. I vosh and feed him. Olga . . she bring him back later.'

As Carver's attempts at pleading with Olga diminished, as the pair got further away, Murphy slumped back down onto the tarpaulins. 'Well if'n that don't beat all,' he said.

Henry laughed, 'Well, Marshal, looks like what you said to Olga last night sure changed the way she looks upon Carver . . . What did you say?'

'Say?' He pointed to Murphy. 'Oh, yes, I follow you now. I simply painted a mental picture in her mind and explained his 'manhood' was substantially more developed than this sorry looking deputy.'

Once again Murphy stood to attention. 'You talkin' about my pecker?' he shouted. 'Now listen here, Marshal, you ain't got no rights to go around telling folk about a man's pecker. That's personal and such. Least of all to Olga! Besides, how would you know about his pecker?'

'I don't, but at least it saved Mister Carver from a certain beating and, if my calculations are correct, I suspect you have just enough time to clean and tidy yourself before Olga discovers what could be the truth and reverses her decision as to who gets a bath.'

Murphy grinned. 'You sure are a smart one, Marshal.'

'And now, if I were you, I would make haste to the hotel. "God does not always smile twice".'

17

CHAPTER 2

The US temperance movement was started in the early 1800s and by the mid-1830s had three-quarters of a million supporters. Carrie Amelia Nation was the woman who brought prohibition to Kansas in 1880, making it the first state to become teetotal.

Carrie was a woman who looked upon strong liquor as the work of the devil and made it her life's ambition to stamp out alcohol, not only in Kansas but also in the whole of the United States. Her methods were draconian, to say the least, because in the early days her most famous demonstration of her displeasure was to rush into a saloon and smash the customer's glasses with a small hatchet before turning her attentions to the fixtures and fittings of the bar.

Despite the rapid growth of the women's temperance movement, Crows Creek had been safe from those ladies, but the success of the temperance campaign in Kansas was slowly oozing its way South and had begun to penetrate the North East part of Texas and thus interfered with the drinking habits of the inhabitants of a town called Cactus Ridge.

Cactus Ridge was not exactly lawless but the authorities had, until recent years, given its population a fair degree of leeway when it came to being rowdy. The reason for this was because there were transient oil workers recruited from any part of the country, drovers with wads of cash passing through and rail workers who compensated being parted from their loved ones by spending all their free time in the saloons and cathouses in the towns they frequented.

The marshal was explaining to Murphy and Carver all about their next mission when the government twins entered Katie's Eating House and sat down at their table.

Murphy gave them a slight smile. 'The marshal was just telling us about Cactus Ridge and how there was some woman who got shot for tryin' to stop folks from havin' nothing more than a friendly drink.'

'Oh dear,' Clarence said. 'I'm afraid it is a little more serious than that. Is this not the case, dear brother?'

'Oh yes,' Claude replied. 'Quite serious, you may say. It would appear there is quite a great deal of unrest in Cactus Ridge and the Women's Temperance League is right in the middle of it all.'

Murphy hammered his massive fist on the table and growled, 'Well, I, for one, don't blame the townsfolk because there ain't nothin' more rilin' than a woman who don't like a man havin' a friendly drink and maybe passin' a few measly cents over a card table every now and then. What do you say, Carver?'

Moses' eyes were glazed in deep thought. 'I saw a woman once. Big woman she was. I remembers it as if it was yesterday.

'I was sittin' mindin' mine own business when she burst into the Dead Elm saloon in Dodge City and tried to spill everybody's drink right onto the floor. . . . Even the best sippin' whiskey that had been specially brought in from the Emerald Isle at over ten dollars a bottle.'

'The hell ya say?' Murphy gasped.

'The hell I do,' he replied knowingly. 'Anyways, on account of the place bein' pretty busy an' all that, plus the dancing girls were showin' their garters and kickin' up a stomp, nobody noticed at first, but as soon as we all knew what was goin' on she was grabbed by the scruff of her neck and throwed out into the street.'

'Was that it?' Murphy gasped again. 'She wasn't tar and feathered?'

'Nope,' Carver replied as he shook his head in disbelief. 'But listen to this: I'd be dad blasted if'n she didn't come right back in and commenced to spillin' more drinks. She even went and spilled mine.'

'What the hell did ya do about that?' Murphy asked.

'Funny you should ask, because she wore a real neat and shiny bonnet. You could tell it was starched or something, but just afore I could snatch it from her head the sheriff must have known what I was goin' to do and he beat me to it. Quick as you like he took it and threw it across the saloon and she went to hurryin' after it. She was grabbin' like she was tryin' to catch the wind but every time she got to where someone was holdin' it they threw it to someone else. Soon every man Jack of us were tossin' her neat little bonnet this way and that until she must have gotten dizzy, because she fell headlong onto the floor right at the feet of the sheriff who, incidentally, was madder than a rattlesnake because it was his sippin' whiskey she done threw away in the first place.'

'I sure bet he was . . . So what did he do next?'

'Well, she took to cryin' and such and the sheriff looked upon her and bent down low. Now I ain't quite certain what he told her because he was talking close into her ear but what he said made her sit up and grin like he'd asked her to marry him.'

'The hell ya say?'

'The hell I do,' Carver replied. 'Next she stood up, dusted herself down and strolled over to the bar; and if'n I live to be two hundred I will never forget the very words she used next.'

'Go on,' Murphy said excitedly.

'She pulled herself close to the barkeep, turned her head away and shouted as loud as she could, "Drinks all round". The place went into uproar as some cowboys jumped behind the bar and took a bottle of whiskey or poured themselves a beer. I tell yer, boys, within a few minutes everyone was toastin' her for her generosity.'

'What did she do next?' Murphy asked.

21

Carver looked from side to side as if he was about to reveal a lost secret. 'She commenced to drinkin' whiskey like a lumberman on a Saturday night. I tell yer, boys, I ain't never seen a woman who could hold her liquor the way that woman could. She must have drunk three bottles of rotgut and still looked as sober as a judge.'

'The hell ya say?'

'The hell I do . . . and by the end of the night she was the only one standin.' He crossed his heart. 'I swear that to be true.'

Murphy rubbed his chin. 'You mean to say all those temperance ladies are set against men drinkin' and such because they want it for themselves?'

'I surely do,' Carver said smugly.

The marshal shook his head in disbelief and gave a pitiful sigh. 'Why must I have to listen to the ramblings of a man whose brain has obviously been fried due to spending too many days in the midday sun without wearing some suitable headgear?' He mumbled to the twins. 'Now, if we may continue?'

'By all means,' Claude said with enthusiasm.

'You go ahead, Marshal,' Clarence added.

'Well, as I was explaining, before I was so rudely interrupted, there is a temperance movement spreading throughout this country and it is growing more powerful by the second. Mostly those in favour of banning alcohol are women but there are certain men in positions of power who see a very real boost to their career if they support this movement. Conversely, there are also certain men in power who see prohibition as a real threat to their livelihood.'

'Prohibition?' Murphy interrupted. 'Sounds like a hangin' offence to me.'

'Oh Lord, give me strength,' Daniel mumbled to the twins before fixing Murphy with a withering stare. 'Prohibition, my dear man, is another term for the banning of alcoholic beverages.'

'Does that include whiskey?' Carver asked.

'What about beer? Does it include beer an' all?' Murphy added.

'Well, of course it does, as well as beer, wine, gin, rum, vodka. . . . In fact, all drinks that need fermentation in order to be produced will be banned if prohibition comes into force.'

'And it's women who want it banned?' Murphy gasped.

'Mostly, but in the main this nation appears to believe alcohol is the root cause for all the violence and immoral behaviour, and that is why the Women's Temperance League is becoming so popular.'

'I don't see what all this has to do with us, Marshal. After all, there's a sheriff in Cactus Ridge, ain't there?' Murphy asked.

Clarence spoke up, 'There was a sheriff, a Sheriff Coulston, and from what I gather he was quite a good sheriff.'

'A very good sheriff by all accounts,' Claude added. 'But he is not there now and things have got rather out of hand since the new sheriff took over.'

'What happened to the old one?' Carver asked.

'Let me guess,' Murphy interrupted. 'Someone

shot him in the back.'

'Not at all,' Clarence pointed out. 'He was voted out of office.'

Murphy rubbed his chin. 'So what's the problem? Who's the new sheriff?'

'A somewhat strange character by the name of Casper Handyside,' Claude answered.

'Old Casper!' Carver blurted out. 'You can't mean Casper Handyside the trapper?'

'From what I gather he may have been a trapper at one time,' Clarence agreed.

'Trapper, buffalo hunter, gold miner and ex-drunk,' Carver explained.

Daniel turned to look at Carver. 'I take it you know this Casper Handyside?'

'Know of him . . . Never met him. Him and his brother used to run an old stagecoach restin' store near to the border; it was called Beaver Skin or some such other name. What they didn't know was the railway came close on by, and there was a railway station with its own store just a few miles from their store so nobody ever visited theirs. From what I was told his brother left and he went slightly crazy: kept on tryin' to kill all the flies in Texas with a bullwhip.'

'How do you know this?' the marshal asked.

'Well, when I was shoving cattle for Dan Bender, we happened to come close to Casper's store. Dusty Miller – he was the cookie who did all our victuals and such – Dusty bought a wagonload of beans and jerky for next to nothing on account of Casper and his brother buyin' too much and not bein' able to get rid.'

'But how do you know so much about Mister Handyside?'

'That's easy. You see, Dusty was one for a story; sometimes he'd have us laughin' so much our ribs would ache. Anyway, one night, he set to telling us about this old-timer called Casper Handyside and how he owned this here store, and how Casper stepped into his own bear trap when he was a trapper, and how he knocked a joist out causin' his mine to come down on his head, and how a buffalo tore a hole in him the size of a fist when he was a buffalo hunter.'

Daniel turned to the twins. 'Have you seen this man?'

They both shook their heads. 'The best we have is in this report,' Claude said as he handed a file to the marshal.

Daniel quickly scanned the report and, without thinking, passed it casually to Murphy, who dropped it on the table as if it were to burn his fingers should he hold it for a second too long. 'Can we be certain this Casper Handyside and the one Carver refers to are one and the same person?' Daniel asked.

Clarence frowned. 'From what we can ascertain there is something of a similarity between the one in the report and the one Carver has heard of, but until you get to Cactus Ridge, one can never be certain.'

'I take it you boys ain't comin' with us?' Murphy asked.

'No indeed,' Claude replied. 'We are staying in Crows Creek and acting as deputies until you all come back.'

Murphy gave a sarcastic laugh. 'And what you two runts goin' to do for firepower?'

'Olga,' Clarence replied. 'She is staying in Crows Creek to look after her ageing mother, and fortunately she has promised to keep an eye on things until you get back, so we shall be quite all right.'

'I'm certain we will,' Claude added.

'I sure hope she don't get to the boil with that big gauge scattergun of hers. You boys won't have the marshal to make her simmer down,' Murphy added mischievously.

Daniel stopped and looked at Murphy. 'Do my ears deceive me? For once I believe you almost managed to speak and keep within the boundaries of the English Language when you used two similar metaphors. We can dismiss "don't" as nothing more than a bad habit but to use "simmer" and "boil" in the same sentence suggests some sort of progress.'

'You sure do talk funny, Marshal,' he said. 'How are we goin' to get to Cactus Ridge?'

'Ah, this is my little surprise for the pair of you, because I have successfully negotiated the purchase of a horse-drawn caravan that will provide me with adequate comfort for the journey. Plus there is ample stowage for some of my more essential equipment, so to speak, and of course quite comfortable sleeping arrangements.'

'And what about us?' Murphy asked.

'I think that's fairly obvious: the both of you will be sleeping under the stars, unless of course you bring

26

some sort of tent along.'

Murphy gave a grunt. 'I don't suppose this here cart of yours drives itself?'

'It most certainly does not. Therefore you will both take turns driving it whilst I sit inside.'

'But us two ain't allowed to sleep in it?'

'If I was to let you or Carver sleep in my caravan, conditions would soon deteriorate to the point they would become intolerable. However, one can tie a horse behind whilst driving and as a special concession I will allow your tent to be lashed to the roof until needed.'

'You're mighty kind, Marshal.'

'Don't mention it. Now, I presume there are certain foods one may take for such a journey. I believe it will take five, six or possibly seven days.'

Murphy grinned. 'Yep . . . hardtack . . . beans . . . jerky . . . plus any rabbit or gopher we may come across.'

'Beans I understand, but I'm afraid I am not familiar with hardtack and jerky.'

'Well, hardtack is a sort of biscuit and jerky is dried beef,' Murphy explained.

'And I presume you are quite used to living on such foods for a period of a short week or so?'

'Done it many times . . . for longer if'n I had to.'

'Admirable. Of course I shall take suitable provisions for myself; I think a savoury pie will last for a while whilst a variety of tinned food will last even longer.'

Murphy quickly glanced at Carver. 'You sure are

good to us, Marshal; whatever would we do without you?'

'Think nothing of it, my good fellows.'

'And I take it if'n we shoot a jackrabbit, or some such other critter, you'll be havin some?'

'That is most kind of you; thank you.' Daniel smiled and began to shuffle excitedly on his chair. 'Do you know, my preliminary thought about undergoing this journey was one of trepidation but now I can see it may be quite a pleasant jaunt. *Tempus fugit,* gentlemen. We shall set out first thing in the morning.'

CHAPTER 3

Dawn arrived with the promise of a glorious day. As the shadows shortened and a gentle breeze began, Murphy saddled Sea Biscuit and led her out from the gloom of the livery stable. It had been quite some time since they were together but they blended like scotch and water, and soon Murphy was happy to be back in the saddle.

Carver's horse was a feisty skewbald mare that he bought from an Apache buck five years earlier. Despite having travelled thousands of miles together, he had never given it a name other than 'low-down horse' or 'mule-faced bag of bones'.

Murphy and Carver came down the main street in opposite directions and met outside the Golden Shoe saloon. 'Where's the marshal?' Carver asked.

'I thought he was with you!' Murphy replied.

'Hell no!'

'Maybe he's gone to get that caravan he was jawin' about?'

'Maybe . . . but he ain't able to drive it.'

29

'Well, who's goin' to drive him?'

'Don't you remember? He said as how both of us could take turns but I got this feelin' there's something he's not telling us. I mean, does he have a horse for this so-called caravan?' Carver asked.

'I know just what you mean. It's like havin' a woodpecker peckin' at the back of my head – something ain't right,' Murphy replied. 'He'd gone afore I woke up so I ain't had the chance to ask him.'

'Where'd he gone?'

'If'n I knew that I'd be on some stage . . . I just told ya, I was asleep when he went.'

'Well, I reckon he'll be at that darn caravan he was crowin' so much about.'

'I reckon you're right . . . You go this way and I'll go that,' Murphy suggested.

'I done come from there and he wasn't there, and you came from over yon' and he wasn't there neither, so where is he then?'

'Good morning, gentlemen!' Daniel said cheerily as he pointed to two grey mares tied outside the Golden Shoe. 'My caravan is behind this very saloon and those are the horses that pull it. Perhaps you would be so kind as to gather them and correctly tether them to the front of my carriage?'

'Hitch, Marshal. . . . You hitch horses to a wagon,' Murphy said as he dismounted and tied Sea Biscuit to the rail. 'Just lead us to it and we'll take over.'

As the three of them went behind the saloon, a vision on wheels came into view. Murphy and Carver stood half in shock, half in disbelief until Murphy broke the silence. 'What in the name of tarnation is that?'

Daniel stood proud as he displayed his mobile home. 'This, gentlemen, is my wonderful caravan.'

'But it looks like a Sideshow Annie done own it,' Murphy gasped.

'Whatever you may mean by that I, shall dismiss as ignorance because this caravan contains all I need for a journey such as the one we are about to embark upon.'

Murphy rubbed his eyes as he looked at every heavily decorated square inch. 'Marshal!' He gasped. 'I don't want to tell yer but this used to be owned by a travelling medicine man, I done seen one just like it in Tulsa. . . . In fact this may be the very same one.'

'There is every chance you could be correct, Deputy, but just think about it. If you are right, this caravan has successfully travelled all over Texas; possibly Arizona, New Mexico and many other territories as well. It has proved to be sound, reliable and safe. I admit the carved gargoyles and gold cherubs may not be to everyone's taste. Neither may the crystal moons and glass stars that hang down from the lace curtained windows, and the words "Webster's Wonder Mix" could cause confusion when one considers there is no Wonder Mix to be found either inside or out, but I must admit I do find it quite charming.'

'Marshal, you can't turn up in that!' Murphy shouted. 'We'll be the laughin' stock of the whole town.'

31

'Nonsense,' Daniel dismissed. 'Now get those horses into place and let us get a move on. *Carpe diem*, gentlemen . . . *Carpe diem.*'

Murphy and Carver hitched up the two grey mares as the marshal went to the rear of the caravan and gained access through the gaily-painted back door. After he had finished, Murphy climbed onto the buckboard reluctantly, took the reins in his hands and gave them a sound slap, but nothing happened. 'Hey-ya!' he shouted, but still nothing happened. 'You two ordinary, no-good mules . . . Do as I tell yer and get goin'.' Again he gave the reins a slap and still both horses remained like stone statues.

Daniel's arm appeared through the purple velvet curtains, passing a shiny silver bell to Murphy. 'Ring this,' he said with a knowing sigh.

'Now, Marshal, what in tarnation do I do with this?'

'Apparently the previous owner trained those horses to respond to the sound of that bell. He was conscious that someone might try and steal his caravan whilst he was plying his trade, so he devised his own security system, so to speak. Therefore I suggest you give it a try and ring it.'

'Aw shucks, Marshal, this ain't funny. Here I am sat on some sort of fortune-teller's wagon, surrounded by silver moons and suchlike, and just to add insult to injury I have to ring this little silver bell so as to get those two stubborn mule-headed horses to move.'

'Just do it, man,' the marshal snapped back.

Reluctantly, Murphy gave the bell a shake and

immediately the greys began to walk forwards slowly. Once again Murphy slapped the reins, but the horses remained walking at the same pace. 'How do I get 'em to get a move on, Marshal?' he shouted.

Daniel's arm appeared for the second time. 'Ring this bell,' he said as he handed Murphy a bigger bell.

'Dad blasted mules ain't worth nothin' but glue, and how do I get 'em to stop?'

'Ah, that's quite simple: you pull back on the reins.'

'How is it you know all this fancy way of handlin' horses, Marshal?'

'The reason I know so much, as you put it, is because I bought the whole outfit from Jack Stoops, the undertaker. Apparently the previous owner came to Crows Creek a few weeks ago suffering from some sort of liver failure, according to the doctor. Quite ironically, it was brought on by the over consumption of his own "elixir of life". Anyway, he knew he was about to die and because he had very little money, he traded this wonderful caravan and horses plus several bottles of Webster's Wonder Mixture for a decent Christian burial.'

'What did Stoops do with all them bottles?'

'Apparently they made wonderful embalming fluid, so he used them in the appliance of his trade.'

As they made slow progress down the main street, Carver rode up to Murphy wearing a large, sarcastic grin. 'You sure look a real picture, Deputy,' he laughed as he slowed his horse to walk alongside. 'You thinking of goin' any quicker, Murphy? We want to be there afore winter.'

Red with embarrassment, Murphy tolled the bigger bell and both horses quickened their pace.

'Well if that don't beat all,' Carver gasped. 'Ringin' that little bell makes 'em move and stuff?'

'It sure does, and when it comes to your turn to do some drivin' you'll feel just as stupid as I do.'

'Have you forgot? I'm the one who knows these here parts like the back of my hand. I know the trails, the waterin' holes, the best places to camp where there ain't no snakes, so I ain't gonna drive that thing.'

'Oh yes, you are.'

'Oh no . . . I . . . ain't.'

'Oh yes, you are.'

'Oh no . . . I . . . ain't.'

'Are too.'

'Children, children, do try to behave,' the marshal shouted from inside. 'We have quite a journey ahead and bickering will not make the miles any shorter. Anyway, whilst you two are outside enjoying the scenery and fresh air, I will take the opportunity to have a little nap . . . although I doubt I will have the chance with you two girls arguing all the time.'

CHAPTER 4

The trail to Cactus Ridge mostly ran along the banks of the Gila River. There were plenty of places to set up camp and, for the first three days of their journey, the weather proved to be kind.

On the fourth day they broke camp just after a dawn that threatened blistering heat, but luckily the river ran in the welcoming shade of Kitchoi Ridge, which kept them quite cool.

A few hours into the day, Daniel decided it was time for his customary nap, so he retired into the back of his caravan and settled down for an hour or two, leaving Murphy to drive and Carver mounted up in front.

Murphy's mind began to wander to times gone by as Carver rode between two large rocks and went out of sight for a moment. The next time he saw Carver, he was sitting astride his horse with his hands in the air. 'Carver!' he shouted. 'What you foolin' at now?'

Carver's head turned slightly backwards. 'This ain't no joke,' he said nervously. 'And I reckon you'd do right to do the same.'

'What do ya think I should do that for?' At that moment his attention was taken by the sound of a lever-action Winchester being cocked and he looked around to see sixteen well-armed Apache Indians holding both he and Carver at gunpoint. Slowly, he raised his hands.

'What do ya think they want, Murphy?' Carver asked.

'Well, they sure ain't come to ask us for a dance,' he moaned.

One young Indian let out a screaming war cry as he somersaulted down skilfully from the top of the left-hand rock. After landing he paused before giving them a confident, beaming smile. 'My name is Soaring Hawk and I speak your tongue,' he said.

'That's good to hear, young fella.' Murphy replied. 'I don't suppose they could lower their weapons? I'm getting mighty nervous.'

The youth shrugged his shoulders as he moved towards Carver. 'They do as they want. Now, give me your gun and belt.' He turned and pointed a finger at Murphy. 'Yours as well.'

With reluctance, Murphy began to unbuckle his rig. 'Better do as he says, Carver; they've got us suckered and outnumbered.'

A leather-faced warrior standing high on the tallest rock shouted something to Soaring Hawk, who nodded in agreement. 'Goyathlay: our leader. He wants to know what is in the wagon.'

'Geronimo?' Murphy blurted out. 'He don't ever

come out of Mexico or New Mexico; what's he doin' here?'

'Right now?' the youth replied as he took their weapons. 'Robbing you, my friend.'

Geronimo beckoned a brave to take Murphy's place and for a second to pull Carver off his horse. 'Now we leave you alone,' Soaring Hawk said with a grin.

'You're leavin' us out here with nothing?' Murphy gasped.

'No . . . we leave you with your lives,' he replied.

'But if'n you leave us out here without food, guns or horses we'll die for sure.' Murphy pleaded.

'I take it you're a Christian?' the youth asked.

'Sure am,' Murphy replied.

'Well, is it not written that God will provide?'

'He ain't goin' to give us food or horses if that's what ya mean.'

Geronimo asked Soaring Hawk a question and in return he replied, causing all the braves to burst out with laughter. 'My leader asks what you want and I tell him you wish to have your weapons, food and horses. This is why we laugh.'

'Well, is there somethin' we can do?' Murphy asked naively.

'Such as?'

'I don't rightly know, but I was once married to a member of the Kiowa tribe and they had some sort of code of honour.'

'We have much honour, my friend.'

Again, Geronimo exchanged a few words with

37

Soaring Hawk. 'Goyathlay, he asks did you ever ride with the Long Knives?'

'To my shame I did for a short while, but after I saw what Custer and his men did to my wife and family, I joined the peace-loving Cheyenne and fought against him good and hard.'

'And Big Horn, you were there?'

Murphy removed his hat, dried the sweat with his handkerchief, held it low in both hands and dropped his head. 'I have to confess, I was there.'

Carver turned in astonishment. 'The hell you say?'

'The hell I do . . . but I wasn't fightin' with the 7th, I was fightin' agen 'em.' As he raised his head his voice filled with pride. 'Custer had it comin' to him; he'd butchered more than a thousand innocent men women and children, including mine . . . Someone had to stop him and I'm proud to have taken part.'

The youth told Geronimo what Murphy had said. The medicine man gave a small respectful bow of his head and told Soaring Hawk to leave them their horses.

'He says from one brave to another, you may keep your horses. Besides, he does not want any trouble here in Texas, but we take your guns and this very fine wagon.' The wagon driver gave out a bloodcurdling scream and slapped the reins on the backs of the greys. As usual, nothing happened.

Murphy gave a reluctant grunt and told the youth about the bells. In turn Soaring Hawk told the braves, who all burst into laughter once more. 'You are a very funny man, my friend,' he said as he

38

vaulted nimbly onto the back of his pony. 'Perhaps we meet again someday.'

A bell rang, then another and the Apaches rode away with the marshal fast asleep in his caravan.

Carver gave a sigh of relief. 'Well, don't that beat all? We're two lucky sons of bitches, I can tell ya that.'

'Lucky?' He pointed in the direction the raiding party had left in. 'They got the marshal, and when they find him they'll skin him alive!'

'That's a fact,' Carver agreed. 'Best hightail it whilst we can, don't want Old Geronimo changing his mind and comin' back now.'

In a wild temper, Murphy threw his hat hard to the ground. 'And I get to go to jail for twenty years.'

'That's if'n they find ya. . . . Maybe you could ride to Mexico, do a little ranchin' there?'

'Maybe you're right!' he shouted with delight, but then his face dropped in disappointment. 'Aw, shucks, I ain't no coward, and I ain't someone who turns his back on a friend neither.'

'But you're free. . . . We both are!'

With great determination, Murphy grabbed Sea Biscuit's reins, put his foot in the stirrup and neatly swung into the saddle. 'If'n I have to, I'll do it all by myself.'

Carver mounted up and pulled next to Murphy. 'You sure are one stupid son of a bitch,' he said. 'You don't stand no chance. There are too many of 'em, and we ain't got no guns.'

Murphy stopped for a while then grinned at Carver. '"We"?' he asked.

Carver shook his head in disbelief. 'That's my problem, always has been, I never knowed when I was well off.'

Murphy gave him a friendly slap on his back. 'Come on, if'n we get after 'em now, we'll soon catch 'em up; them havin' to go as fast as that cart will go an' all.'

'What then?' Carver asked.

'We'll wait until nightfall and break the marshal free.'

'How do we know they won't kill him when they find him? You know yourself, the marshal can get pretty annoyin'.'

'They won't; they'll have a bit of fun with him first. I know Apache ways.'

'OK, Murphy, I hope you knows what you're doin'. . . . Let's get ridin'. Hey, maybe they'll just cut out his tongue. God does move in mysterious ways.'

From a safe distance they followed the Apaches' trail until they came to a narrow gap in the hills that led to a small canyon. Murphy rubbed his chin in thought. 'I reckon they'll be hauled up in there.' ❦

Carver raised himself in the saddle and looked around. 'I don't know all the trails around here, but from what I can see I reckon you're right.'

Murphy gave a nod of agreement. 'Best we stay here until dark and then climb up this ridge. Maybe from there we'll be able to see what's goin' on.'

'Sounds good to me.' Carver looked at the position of the sun. 'Sundown won't be for a few hours yet, so I'm goin' to haul up under those trees over yon.'

Murphy agreed as he dismounted and went through his saddlebags. 'At least we've got water and some jerky.'

Carver jumped down, grinned and took out a bottle from his saddlebag. 'And a little sippin' whiskey,' he said as he shook the bottle playfully.

'Well, don't that beat all?' Murphy added. 'We'll have us a little party. Maybe a hand or two of poker?'

'Without no guns, maybe it could be our last. Who knows?' Carver said solemnly.

'I reckon you could be right, but whatever happens that still ain't no reason to cheat,' Murphy added.

'I ain't never cheated at cards.'

Murphy laughed as he placed a cheroot in the corner of his mouth. 'Me neither, so let's get to playin'.'

Together they drank and played cards until dark arrived. 'Time to go,' Murphy said.

'I'm with you, partner,' Carver agreed.

As they hauled their way up the ridge, small stones cascaded down, rattling as they bounced to the bottom. 'Sure wish we didn't make so much noise,' Murphy whispered. 'I heard that an Apache can here a horse fart in the next state.'

'Likely smell it too,' Carver gasped as he pulled himself to the top of the ridge.

As Murphy came up next to him they could see the Indian camp quite clearly. Seven tepees were arranged in a rough circle around a central camp-

fire. Twenty or twenty-five braves were sitting in the
light of the fire and a string of thirty or so tethered
ponies could be seen in the distant half-light.
Wearing a ceremonial headdress, there was what
appeared to be a medicine man dancing around the
fire keeping all the braves enthralled with magic. On
his naked hand he held a flame which he threw into
the air and changed its colour as he caught it again.
Next he produced an arrow, which appeared to float
and dance in front of him and then broke an egg
from which a tiny bird flew away.

'That medicine man sure is keeping 'em spell-
bound,' Murphy whispered. 'Maybe that'll give us a
chance to sneak down and find the marshal.'

'Well, I can't see him anywhere.' Carver replied. 'I
reckon he'll be dead by now.'

Suddenly, Murphy tapped Carver on the shoulder.
'There's his caravan over there. Maybe they ain't
found him yet.'

'Maybe, but we ain't in no position to do owt about
it right now.'

Before Murphy could turn to see what Carver was
talking about he felt the cold steel blade of a knife at
his throat.

'Slowly does it, Carver; I reckon we're in trouble
agen.'

The deputies rose carefully to their feet and began
to walk down towards the Indian camp. As they
appeared in the light of the fire all became silent and
motionless until Soaring Hawk came forward. 'I see
we do meet again, my friend,' he said. Next he

looked at Geronimo, who spoke to him in Apache. 'It is not good. He tells me you will die a thousand painful deaths.'

Murphy held out his hands in explanation. 'Now wait just a moment, young fella. I can explain why we came here. We didn't mean you no harm; we just wanted our friend back.' He pointed to the caravan. 'The one who was in there.'

Soaring Hawk spoke to the medicine man, who placed a death mask on his face before he began to chant. Whilst rotating on the spot he picked up a spear, brandished it before them and threw it into the ground. He took out some blue powder from a pouch, blew it in their faces and screamed to the Gods.

Slowly and with much menace, he took off his mask, ceremonial headdress and robe. 'Good evening, gentlemen,' Daniel said with a smile.

Murphy and Carver stood speechless as the Apaches rolled about in fits of laughter. 'Marshal!' he exclaimed. 'Why, you stupid son of a bitch, you nearly had Carver and me crappin' our pants.'

'Speak for yourself,' Carver said, trying to regain his dignity. 'I knew it was the marshal all the time.'

With furrowed brow, Murphy fixed Moses with a steely stare. 'You did not!'

'I surely did.'

'Did not.'

'Did too.'

'Gentlemen, gentlemen,' Daniel interrupted as he continued to grin. 'I really must point out that whilst you thought you were following them, two braves doubled back and followed you.' He pointed to the top of the ridge. 'Five lookouts saw you coming and they watched as you drank and played cards. They even took your horses without you knowing. Gentlemen, this whole elaborate charade was for your benefit, because I must admit Goyathlay is a very wise leader indeed.'

After the excitement had died down, Geronimo spoke to Soaring Hawk. 'Goyathlay,' he shouted. 'He says you are welcome to stay and leave tomorrow. You may have your weapons back and he wishes you go in peace.'

Daniel gave a respectful bow as Murphy's red face became redder with rage. 'How come they didn't skin you alive? And right now I wish they had.'

'I must admit that when they discovered me in my caravan I was somewhat concerned, but after I showed them my small collection of fine wines and three bottles of five star Napoleon brandy, I realised there was some common ground to cover.'

'But why didn't they just take the brandy and kill ya for it?'

'Perhaps they may have done just that but thankfully, as they dragged me out, I noticed one of the braves had a wound that had gone quite bad and therefore had a high temperature as a result. He was noticeably shivering and yet sweating at the same time. I explained I was a physician of sorts and I had some powder and cream that would help the poor man.'

44

'And did ya?'

'Oh yes. You see I have a good selection of healing medicines that I keep in the small drawers of my caravan. Firstly I administered a powder containing willow bark, which reduced the man's temperature almost straight away; next I applied a balm that was discovered a few years ago in Spain. Nobody fully understands how it works, but some stable lads had been applying it to open wounds with remarkable results. It comes from a fungal growth, mixed with the sweat where the leather and brass of the horse's tethers come into contact with the creature's skin. It is almost magical.'

'And what was all that magic you were doin'?'

'Ah, the art of prestidigitation was taught to me by an ancient Indian Fakir.'

Carver wagged his finger at Daniel. 'Now, Marshal, that ain't fair . . . If'n he helped you like you said, you ought not bad-mouth him like you have, no matter what tribe he's from – unless'n he's Crow, of course. I was once in the Northern Territories and I got cheated by a flathead over two young colt painters. I didn't know this but he'd painted one to look like the other, and days later we got caught in the rain and it washed clean off.'

Daniel gave an audible tut. 'Are you two related in any way?'

'What'll you mean, Marshal?' Carver asked.

'Well, every time I mention India or an inhabitant of that great country, you assume I am talking about some random Native American.' He reached out at

Carver's ear and from within produced a silver dollar. 'This is the art of prestidigitation – magic, as you call it, or sleight of hand if you prefer. It is to deceive the eye, or prove the hand is quicker than the eye.'

'And those Apaches thought you had the power of a real medicine man?' Murphy asked.

Daniel gave a sigh. 'How primitive do you think they are? For your information, Deputy, they did not think anything of the sort. It was my idea to entertain them, and a very appreciative audience they turned out to be.'

Murphy's eyes narrowed. 'Well, what about all that dancing and those feathers and such?'

'Goyathlay's idea. His braves knew where you were but Goyathlay appears to be able to work out another person's actions long before they take place. It is a most remarkable gift, and one which has kept him ahead of the Mexican army for quite a few years now.'

'And that young buck Soaring Hawk? He told Geronimo what you were saying?'

'That appeared to be the case, but I am convinced that Geronimo, as you call him, understands English quite well but prefers not to let it become common knowledge.'

'And what are they doin' here?' Murphy asked.

'Their motive is one of revenge, I'm afraid,' the marshal sighed. 'A band of Mexican bandits slaughtered many inhabitants of an Apache village and these braves are on their trail.'

'From what Carver and me have seen, those

Mexicans are as good as dead.'

'Quite so, but for tonight, gentlemen, I shall bid you goodnight, for we leave first thing in the morning.'

When dawn arrived, the marshal and his deputies awoke to find all the Chiricahua Indians had left, almost without a trace, leaving Sea Biscuit and the other horses tied up. Their guns and rigs were hanging from the saddle pummels.

CHAPTER 5

Cactus Ridge stood at the base of a slowly rising hill comprised of sparse chaparral, so sparse there was nothing for cattle to graze on. Only a few birds, lizards and snakes managed to eke a living on the insects and cactus flowers that thrived there. In contrast, the long plain that drifted east was lush, green and ripe due to it being fed by a freshwater spring that split into five small streams.

The town itself bordered the main north-south trail and, from a distance, looked like a giant multi-coloured snake. It had no depth, no side streets, nothing other than building after building placed unimaginatively next to one another. To make things worse, one saloon was at the northern end and the other at the southernmost point, so that visitors approaching from the north patronised the Ace in the Hole saloon and those from the south's first visit was always to the Last Trading Post Hotel.

Carver pulled up outside the Last Trading Post, dismounted and tethered his horse to the rail outside whilst Murphy put the brakes on the marshal's caravan. 'This is it, Marshal,' he shouted as he jumped down, stretched his back, yawned and gazed at the building with surprise. 'Oh-wee! If this don't beat all,' he screamed. 'It all looks a bit fancy to me, Marshal.'

Daniel emerged from his caravan through a gold inlaid carved redwood door, stood back and examined the building's architecture. 'My word, this is a surprise.'

The Last Trading Post Hotel's design was based on villas found around the Mediterranean Sea. Finished in magnolia, two imitation marble pillars held up a hibiscus-covered porch, next to which four rectangular windows containing bull's eye glass stood here and there atop heavily flowered window boxes. The second storey was surrounded by a pink veranda, on which there was several standard rose trees planted in polished brass pots with embossed figurines of ancient Greek warriors locked in combat. The roof was covered in terracotta tiles, through which appeared two brilliant white chimneystacks.

As Murphy grabbed a suitcase in each hand and swung towards the hotel door he looked at Carver and grinned. 'Sure has been a long day; I'm drier than tumbleweed in a sand storm.'

'Come, come, gentlemen, the time for liquid libation is after we have registered in the hotel and all my luggage is stacked neatly in my room.' He clapped his hands like a strict schoolmistress. 'So come on, I will take care of the preliminaries, such as introductions and paperwork, whilst you both concentrate on the more menial tasks.'

The Last Trading Post was built on the site of a small trading post that was set up during the late 1700s. The original was nothing more than a wooden cabin, the purpose of which was to provide somewhere for trappers to sell their furs and stock up with biscuits, beans, rotgut and tobacco, but as Cactus Ridge developed, the Last Trading Post underwent a process of metamorphoses from which emerged a colourful establishment, noted for having high class rooms, good food and most excellent service. In contrast, the Ace in the Hole catered for the less discerning customer and provided gambling, beer and whiskey, bucket spittoons and ladies of spurious character.

Daniel gave a sigh of satisfaction as he donned his fedora, took his silver-topped cane in his left hand and turned the brass knob on the hotel door. Inside to the right he laid his eyes on red velvet drapes, which hung down across the entrance to a spiral staircase. Before the staircase was an open plan doorway leading to the restaurant, and before that a reception desk with walnut panels fitted snugly in the corner next to the lace-curtained window. Behind the desk stood a man in his early fifties with a thin face, white hair and a red silk waistcoat over a pink and grey striped shirt. His demeanour suggested he managed the hotel. He pointed a crooked finger of approval at Daniel's caravan as he rolled his eyes.

His words came out faster than a Gatling gun. 'Oooh, I positively adore your method of transport.

It's so very you.' Looking Daniel up and down he gave a cheeky smile and pursed his lips. 'I can guess who you are . . . You are the English marshal and we've been expecting you for days now, but I suppose beggars can't be choosers when the devil pays the piper.'

Daniel gave a small bow in acknowledgement. 'Indeed, I was informed you were expecting us.' He gave his hand in friendship only to receive a limp handshake in return. 'Daniel Wheetman at your service,' he said.

'Jason Monkshood, but friends call me Jay and, as you're staying in my most wonderful hotel, I shall consider you to be a friend.' As he described his hotel as wonderful, his hands encompassed the entire interior with pride. 'Now I have a reservation for you and two other gentlemen.' He reached for a set of keys from a board behind. 'Number six. It's very comfortable with views across the hills, It has its own bath and a double size four-poster bed.' He placed a register in front of Daniel. 'Now, in your best handwriting, please fill in the details.'

As Daniel was completing the register, Murphy and Carver came banging roughly through the door with some of his luggage. 'Where do ya want this stuff, Marshal?'

Jay held his cheeks in delight. 'Now these must be the other gentlemen I am expecting, and I must say they're both very big boys.' Next he picked up a silver bell daintily and gave it a neat little shake. 'Lorenzo!' he shouted. 'Lorenzo! Oh, where is that boy? I swear some days I have to do everything myself.' As he waited, two stout ladies came from the restaurant behind him and placed bonnets on their heads before collecting their parasols. 'Ladies, you both look exquisite today,' he remarked whilst wearing a beaming smile. 'Navy blue is really your colour, Mavis; it can make me look a little peaky but on you it brings out the very best.' After the ladies had left he lifted the right side of his mouth in a fake snarl. 'Navy blue makes her look like a beached whale; I don't know why she wears it. Someone should tell her . . . and as for Miss Blake with the blonde hair, well, I bet you a dollar to a pound of sherbet the collar doesn't match the cuffs.'

As he spoke, a swarthy-looking man came from the restaurant carrying a stack of dirty plates, looking quite flustered as he tried to smarten himself up in front of Jay. '*Sí*, Señor Jason?' he asked.

'Ah, Lorenzo,' Jay began. 'Take this gentlemen's luggage to room six.'

'*Sí señor.*'

Daniel turned to smile at Lorenzo. '*¿Cómo está usted?*' he asked.

'*Sí señor.*'

'Errr, Lorenzo?' the marshal asked. 'May I ask you a personal question?'

'*Sí señor.*'

'Do you speak any Spanish?'

Lorenzo put the plates down on a vacant table and approached close to the marshal. 'Hardly a word,' he whispered.

'Then why do you pretend to be Spanish?'

'It is not my idea,' Lorenzo replied. 'I was born in America but my parents were from Finland, so I speak Finnish quite well. Anyway, I read tales about the Wild West in dime store comics so I moved out here for adventure. Unfortunately the only work I could find is as a waiter; not much adventure there.'

'So why does he want you to pretend you are Spanish?'

Lorenzo cautiously looked from side to side. 'So the ladies will speak and think I do not understand them; this way Jason can keep up with all the gossip.'

Jason's curiosity got the better of him. 'Now what's this boy telling you, Marshal?'

'Well, it is obvious he cannot speak Spanish. I was asking him why he should pretend to be able to, and he informs me the subterfuge is so he is able to get close to your customers whilst they speak freely.'

Jason waved his hands in alarm. 'Oh, please keep your voice down! These are very difficult times.' He came close to Daniel and pointed to his restaurant. 'Most of the ladies in there form the temperance movement. Normally it doesn't bother me because my hotel is teetotal, but of late there has been a certain increase in tension between the temperance movement and those who partake in the consumption of whiskey and such, so I consider it my duty to keep an eye on things.'

'I find what you are saying to be quite bizarre. I don't understand. . . . Why can he not pretend to be from Finland? Doesn't that make more sense?'

53

Jason curled his face in disagreement. 'No, because I speak a little Spanish and I intend to teach him.'

'Why could Lorenzo not teach you Finnish?' Daniel asked.

'Finnish! Have you heard it? It's a language all of its own, completely indecipherable, rather like Apache or Sioux. It would be easier to learn how to speak chickenhawk. No . . . . Spanish it is.'

Murphy cleared his throat. 'Ahem. Marshal, where do ya want these bags? Me and Carver are getting mighty thirsty. Seven days we've been eatin' dust.'

'Oooh, get him with his high and mighty attitude,' Jason said. 'Lorenzo will take care of them and then get you some tea or coffee.'

'Tea or coffee? We don't want no coffee! What we want is a nice, cool beer.' Carver insisted.

With rapid indignation, Jason drew himself to his full height of five foot five. 'Not in here, you won't,' he said as he turned his back on Murphy and Carver. 'Now if it's liquor you want, be gone to the Arse in the Hovel. They cater for fellow ruffians who do not care if their bed has bugs and their food is served on the floor. I provide the very best care, the very best attention, the very best rooms, the very best food and the very best service.' He scowled at Lorenzo, who was struggling to gather Daniel's suitcases. 'Just as soon as I get him trained, that is.'

Daniel stepped forward and stopped Lorenzo. 'Please leave them, my good fellow. My deputies will deal with the luggage. I trust you have unfinished

54

work in the restaurant?'

Lorenzo dropped his head and mumbled as he walked away. 'Unfinished in the restaurant, in the kitchen, in the bedrooms . . . Adventure is what I came out west for and look what I have found.'

Jason gave a tut as he folded his arms. 'Why, the ungrateful. . . .'

'Deputies,' the marshal interrupted as he passed Murphy a key. 'Please take those suitcases to my room.'

'We ain't your slaves, Marshal,' Murphy insisted as both he and Carver picked up Daniel's luggage reluctantly and began to climb the stairs. Murphy grinned and shook his head. 'That Jason sure greases the ladies good and proper. He reminds me of a sideshow pimp.'

'It's the third room on the right,' they heard Jason shout just as three ladies appeared through the front door. 'Oooh, ladies,' he screeched. 'You all look more radiant every day . . . Lorna, honey, that dress simply does it. . . . No, wait, you must be Lorna's younger sister . . . and Safire, I bet half the men in town are simply swooning after you in that hat; and Lucy, dear . . . as usual, you look simply divine.' He clapped his hands. 'I'll make certain Lorenzo has your table ready; just go through.' After they had gone he mumbled under his breath to Daniel. 'Mutton done up as lamb, all three of them . . . Did you see Lorna's dress? It makes me wonder what she's doing for curtains. Safire's hat looks like some Billy goat had chewed it first, and if Lucy's backside gets any bigger I shall have to reinforce my furniture.' He rolled his eyes, took back the register and began to check Daniel's details. 'Not married, I see?' he said as he placed his bony hand on Daniel's. 'We must see what we can do about that, you naughty boy.'

'I am married to my work,' the marshal replied as he pulled his hand back. 'Which brings me to the reason we came to Cactus Ridge in the first place. What can you tell me about the lady who was murdered?'

Jason put his horrified hand on his heart. 'I hope you don't think we had anything to do with it!'

'We?' the marshal asked. 'Who is "we"?'

'Of course, you haven't met my partner in crime.' He gave a girlish giggle. 'Lawrence is his name. Together we own this wonderful hotel. He's out at the minute. A lawyer, you understand; no doubt he'll have his head buried in some legal matter or other. His office is almost next door.'

'A lawyer?' Daniel remarked. 'Did you buy this hotel first or did he set up in practice first?'

'No, we both came to town looking for adventure and Lawrence set up his practice almost straight away. We lived in this very building until one day it became vacant. It wasn't what you see today; it was very different, my dear. Drab, drab and drab . . . but we soon made one or two changes for the better and, hey presto, it is as you see it now.'

'And the Mediterranean look, whose idea was that?'

56

'We both had the same idea, and that was to copy a place we once stayed at when we were in Rome – that's in Italy, you know – and from our balcony we could see the Parthenon and the hills beyond.'

'Surely you mean the Forum?'

'What did I say?'

'You said the Parthenon.'

'Silly me; I'd forget my own head if it wasn't sewn on.'

'And of course you must have visited the Acropolis?'

'Many times.'

Murphy and Carver came back down the stairs. 'We've left them bags on the floor, Marshal. . . . Woo-wee, you sure have a fancy room.' He looked at Jason. 'Hey, fella, where's our rooms?'

Jason gave a light, unconcerned sniff. 'Yours are at the back. I believe it's what you term a bunkhouse; quite waterproof and serviceable.' He turned to the marshal and smiled. 'Before we managed to attract a more discerning customer we had to put up with cowboys and other such ruffians; your deputies will be fine, I'm certain.'

Murphy glared at Jason. 'Now listen here, you low-down varmint: Carver and me ain't cowboys no longer, and if'n it wasn't for the fact we have to keep a real good watch on the marshal we'd tell ya to take your fancy little hotel and shove it where the sun don't shine. First, you don't serve no beer nor whiskey, then you tell us we have to stay in the bunkhouse. You're getting my dander up, do ya hear?'

'My, my . . . anger does become you,' Jason squeaked. 'But there is only one room available and the marshal has that.'

'The bunkhouse is fine,' Carver interrupted as he gave Murphy a sly wink. 'We'll be just fine.'

'There's no lock on the door,' Jason explained. 'Gather your luggage and make yourself at home, boys.'

Murphy stood for a while then followed Carver outside. 'What in the name of tarnation did you say that for? I had that white-haired popinjay right where I wanted him.'

'Shhh! Keep your voice down,' Carver whispered as he looked to see who could hear. 'He don't allow no booze, right?'

'Right.'

'And those women he's panderin' to don't allow none either, right?'

'And we wants some, right?'

'Right.'

'So if'n we was to sneak out to the saloon over yon and we were havin' to use that fancy staircase every five minutes, he'd know when we was comin' and goin', but when we're out back, as he puts it, he won't know nothing.'

Murphy's face lit up. 'Carver, I reckon you're right. Let's get our saddle-bags and take the horses over to the livery stable. I feel a mighty thirst a-comin'.'

After they had seen to the horses and thrown their saddle-bags onto two cots in the bunkhouse, they walked slowly towards the Ace in the Hole. Making most of their deputy badges, they wore them high and proud as they tipped their hats to passing towns-folk, giving the occasional 'Ma'am', or 'Sir' as it pleased them until they stood outside the saloon and Murphy gave a satisfied grin. 'This is more like it,' he said as they listened to the piano music mixed with the sound of clinking glasses and laughter. 'I'm goin' to get me a long tall beer, and if'n they have steak and potatoes, those too.'

'Whiskey for me. . . . Just the good stuff,' Carver said as they pushed through the swinging half doors and entered the building.

The bar was situated to their left, whilst tables and chairs covered every inch of the floor; right the way to the piano player on the far right. The air hung heavy with tobacco smoke as the unmistakable smell of beer and whiskey floated into their welcoming nostrils. 'Sure looks good to me,' Murphy grinned as they found a place at the crowded bar.

'What'll it be, gents?' the slim, greasy-haired barkeep asked.

'Two beers, a bottle and two glasses,' Murphy replied.

'Two beers, a bottle and two glasses comin' right up, gents.'

As the barkeep poured the beers they both watched with satisfied expectancy and, as he pushed them forward, they both watched the tiny silver bubbles rise through the golden liquid until they formed rich foam on the top. 'Here goes nothing, Carver,' Murphy said as they both took four or five gulps before wiping the foam from their lips.

Carver turned and leaned with his back to the bar. 'Can't see no food,' he said.

Murphy beckoned to the barkeep. 'Yes, sir?' he asked.

'Don't you serve food here?'

'No call for it,' he replied cheerily. 'Folks around here frequent the Baptist Tabernacle; they do a mighty good meal for fifty cents.'

'Is that a hotel?' Murphy asked.

'No. . . . It's what it says, a Baptist Tabernacle.'

'You mean with preachers an' all?'

'Sure thing, but they ain't pushy. They may say a prayer or two or sing a hymn, but folks around here have gotten used to it and sort of go along with it.'

Murphy rubbed his chin. 'Fifty cents, ya say?' The barkeep nodded in return as he placed a bottle and two glasses on the bar. 'Much obliged,' Murphy said as a voice from the past rang out.

'Moses Carver. . . . Well I'll be a son of a gun. . . . Is that you?'

As Carver looked through the smoke, his eye narrowed at first, then a beaming smile came over his face. 'Klondike. . . . What in the name of blazes are you doin' here?'

A small, frail old man dressed in dirty dungarees drew closer. His beard and moustache were stained yellow from nicotine and framed his almost toothless mouth. 'Don't ask about me because I heard as you went to Arkansas herdin' beef for some rich cattleman?'

60

'And last I heard of you, you were digging more holes than a grain house rat in California. Did you ever hit the mother load?'

'Never did.'

'Hey, Klondike,' he said as he polished up his tin star. 'Meet Murphy. . . . Me and him are deputy marshals.'

Klondike squinted hard at Murphy. 'Ain't I seen you somewhere before, young fella?'

'Don't recall.'

'Strange, I never forget a face. . . . Wait a minute, didn't you scout for Custer?'

'Yep.'

'I know who you are now. I saw you one day when I was pannin' for gold in an old crawfish river. Custer and his Yankee soldiers came a-ridin' by. All slickered up they were, with old Yellow Hair himself up front, and they made camp nearby. I remember you because you were tied up as some sort of prisoner and they left you in the blazin' sun. By gobs, you looked real thirsty.' He shook his head in disbelief. 'I wouldn't treat a dog like that, so after nightfall I snook around behind and gave you a drink. I even loosened those ropes around your wrists . . . Didn't stick around to find out how you did; I just hightailed it.'

Murphy's face lit up with delight. 'That was you?' he asked. 'Why, I can still taste that water today. I reckon I owe you my life, old-timer. If'n you hadn't done what you did for me, I'd be a dead man by now . . . Murphy's the name.'

61

'Well, Murphy, I don't know what you'd done to get them to truss you up and all, and I reckon it ain't none of my business, but I'm sure glad I helped; you bein' a friend of Carver's an' all.'

Murphy took Klondike's hand and shook it in gratitude. 'If'n there's anything I can do for you, you don't have to ask, consider it done.'

'I'll keep that in mind, but first you can tell me what you're doin' in Cactus Ridge.'

'We're with this English marshal. He's over at the Last Trading Post, and to tell you the truth we ain't quite sure as to what it is he's doin'. Our job is to watch his back, that's all.'

'English, you say?'

'English . . and a pain in the butt.'

Suddenly a weathered-faced cowboy standing at the end of the bar shouted out. 'Hey, Deputies, you wearin' those tin stars so as to get your heads blown off?'

Murphy fixed him with his eyes. 'Friend,' he began. 'Just havin' a friendly drink, that's all.'

The man and two cowboys came up close. 'The law ain't welcomed around here; they leave a kinda smell. Don't ya think so, boys?'

The other two gave a forced laugh, as Murphy stood pan-faced. 'We don't want any trouble, boys. What can we get ya?' he said.

The weathered man pushed a cheroot between his teeth and grinned. 'Light me,' he said menacingly.

Murphy took a deep breath, struck a match on the bar and lit the man's cheroot. 'As I said, boys, we're

62

just havin' a friendly drink.'

The man took their bottle, poured himself a large whiskey and downed it in one. 'I reckon you've finished with this,' he said as he poured himself another.

Carver's temper began to boil as he flipped the leather loop from the hammer of his colt slowly. 'That ain't friendly, boys,' he drawled, but Murphy grabbed his arm.

'Simmer down, Moses,' he said with a smile.

Suddenly Klondike stepped between them. 'Now come on, boys, these here two deputies are friends of mine. This one is Moses Carver and this gent I only knows as Murphy.'

One of the other cowboys whispered in the weathered man's ear and his face changed to one of fear. 'You're Moses Carver?' he asked.

'Yep.'

'Sorry about the mix-up, boys,' he said with a quiver in his voice. 'Here .. er. . . . Let me get you another bottle.'

The barkeep, who had been keeping an eye on things, slapped another bottle on the bar. 'Thank you, boys,' he said. 'Sometimes things get a little out of hand around here when some of the cowboys want to let off steam.'

Murphy pushed the new bottle aside, asked for four more glasses and poured six drinks. 'To the South!' he toasted.

'To the South!' they replied.

As the afternoon became evening and evening

became night, Murphy, Carver, Klondike and the three cowboys carried on drinking until the saloon started to close. 'Food!' Murphy shouted. 'Food. That's what I want. A whole mess of potatoes and a rare steak.'

'You ain't goin' to find nowhere open at this time of night,' the barkeep said as he collected their glasses. 'It's gone nine.'

'Ain't you got nothing?' Murphy asked.

'Pickled eggs, and there's some hardtack a drover left behind,' he replied.

'*That*, my friend,' he slurred, 'will have to do.'

'We got a jackrabbit that ain't began to turn,' the weathered man said as he slumped into a chair and pointed towards the door. 'It's on my saddle, the bay mare; help yourself.'

Carver put the jar of eggs under one arm and grabbed the bag of hardtack as Murphy threw a few silver dollars on the counter. 'Mighty nice drinkin' with ya boys,' he said as he wobbled towards the door.

Outside, Murphy took the dead jackrabbit from the saddle and both he and Carver swayed towards the bunkhouse. 'Shhh. Try to be quiet,' he whispered as they neared the Last Trading Post. 'Don't wake anyone up.'

'Hey, Murphy,' Carver said. 'There's a lantern hangin' up there. Maybe we should light it and that way we won't disturb no one.'

Murphy gave a drunken nod as he took it down and applied a match to it. Inside there was no one else. 'Hey, we got the place to ourselves,' he said.

64

'Carver, you light the stove and I'll skin this critter.'

Carver looked inside the stove. 'There's plenty of firewood but we ain't got no kindlin'.'

Murphy picked up a black can and gave it a sniff. 'Use some of this coal oil.'

Carver emptied the can of oil into the stove, took a lighted match and dropped it inside. Without warning, a huge explosion lifted him off his feet and threw him onto a cot. Murphy dashed forwards and began to smash the flames with a dry dusty blanket, which soon caught fire.

'Get some water.' Murphy shouted.

'I can't see none anywhere.' Carver hollered back.

Pointing to the jar of pickled eggs Murphy yelled. 'Use that!'

Carver threw the jar at the stove, which shattered and allowed two-dozen rubbery eggs to scatter high and low, one of which hit the lantern and knocked it to the ground, causing more flames to spread across the floor.

'This ain't no place for us!' Murphy shouted. 'Let's grab our gear and hightail it.'

'Fire! Fire!' they shouted as they ran around without a clue what to do. Soon several townsfolk came to find out what the commotion was as the flames got higher and higher until the bunkhouse became a complete inferno. Using the shadows for cover, Murphy and Carver sneaked away quietly.

CHAPTER 6

The bunkhouse fire caused most of the hotel guests to get limited amounts of sleep, but Murphy and Carver slept the sleep of the dead in the livery stable. The marshal was at breakfast when they joined him in the restaurant.

'Mornin', Marshal,' Murphy said as he and Carver sat down. 'Lovely day.'

Daniel fixed them with a withering stare and began to whisper. 'Now listen here, the both of you. Taking into account your *modus operandi*, I have been making enquiries about the incident that took place last night behind this very building, and I am certain you know more than a little about this blatant act of arson.'

Murphy sat up and looked stunned. 'Us, Marshal?' he asked with great indignation. 'We don't know nothin' about no fire.'

The marshal began to smile. 'Perhaps you would define the term "arson"?'

'We don't know what you mean, Marshal?' Carver added.

'Arson! What does it mean?'

Murphy rubbed his chin in thought. 'I reckon it means fire. What about you, Carver?'

'I agree.'

'So you do understand what I am talking about when I refer to a deliberate act of arson?'

'Sure do, Marshal,' Murphy agreed with a grin.

'And you insist you had nothing to do with it?'

'Not Carver and me, that's for sure.'

'Then perhaps you wouldn't mind telling me where you went last night?'

'You got us there, Marshal. We admit we did succumb to the evils of drink and went for a small beer over at the Ace in the Hole. We sort of stayed until dark. . . . Anyways, as we saw it – and not wantin' to wake anyone – we decided it would only be fair if'n we slept over at the livery stable. Ain't that so, Carver?'

'That's so,' he agreed.

'And you never returned to the bunkhouse the whole evening?'

Murphy gazed towards the ceiling in false thought. 'Errr, let me think. Nope, don't reckon we did.'

'What about you, Carver?' the marshal asked.

'I seem to recall we never came close, Marshal, and that's the truth.'

'Do either of you know what a lagomorph is?'

The deputies took the time to look at one another and shook their heads. 'Don't reckon we do,

Marshal,' Murphy said innocently.

'There's a stage coach to Largo,' Carver added proudly.

'That's true, Carver . . . maybe it's somethin' to do with the Largo Stage, Marshal, but for the life of me I thought you knew just about everythin' there is to know. Maybe this Jason fella who owns this here hotel knows?'

Daniel gave out a long sigh. 'For your information, gentlemen, a lagomorph is a small furry creature with a dentition formula that sets it aside from rodents. The genus contains rabbits and hares, one of which you were given last night, along with a jar of pickled eggs and some hardtack. Now, sieving through the debris after the fire, I discovered all three. I must admit the hardtack was rather difficult to identify but the other two items you brought into the bunkhouse were not. In short, you two burned down the bunkhouse and I know it.'

Murphy raised his hands in protest. 'Now wait a minute, Marshal, it were an accident. We didn't mean to burn it down; it just happened.'

The marshal leaned closer so as to keep his voice down. 'Is it not enough we left Crows Creek in a state of destruction, without the pair of you bringing your unique brand of misfortune upon this fair town? I mean just look at it, we've not yet managed to spend a whole day here and so far you two have managed to destroy a small part of it; give it a week and the possibilities are endless.'

'Aw, come on, Marshal,' Murphy pleaded. 'All we

did was try to light the stove.'

'Try to light the stove, indeed! When I examined the ashes, the only thing that wasn't still warm was the stove.'

'But, Marshal, it was just bad luck, that's all.' Murphy's eyes grew wide as he thought of something that offered a glimpse of redemption. 'Anyway, I just thought of somethin'. Last night Carver and me went to the saloon. That much you do know, but what ya don't know is we were jawed at something terrible and we both kept our cool.'

Carver banged on the table in agreement. 'That's true, Marshal. These three cowboys came a-pushin' us because we were lawmen. They were sayin' as how the law ain't welcome here.'

'That's the honest truth, Marshal.' Murphy added. 'So don't that explain why they have Old Casper as sheriff?'

'Most certainly it goes someway to confirm my beliefs,' Daniel agreed. 'But I already had the situation worked out in the first place, so it was quite unnecessary for you to pursue your own form of puerile investigation.'

Murphy looked at Carver and rubbed his chin. 'I ain't certain if'n if he means we did good nor bad?'

'I ain't either.'

'Listen carefully, Deputies. It does not matter whether you are right or wrong; the main thing is to keep a low profile at all times and not bring too much attention to yourselves. We have very little idea as to who does what in this town and to whom they do it, and until we do please try not to destroy any more of it.'

'Shucks, Marshal, there you go agen. We already told ya it was an accident!'

'Please keep your voice down,' the marshal pleaded. 'Our genial host is about to come and take our order.'

'I expect you boys have heard?' Jason asked innocently.

Murphy put on his very best concerned expression. 'The marshal has told us all about the fire an' all,' he said. 'Any idea as to what happened?'

'I have my suspicions,' he said as he pursed his lips and nodded his head. 'But wild horses wouldn't drag it from me. I mean, I don't want to go around spreading false rumours about him who runs that den of iniquity at the end of town.'

'You mean the Ace in the Hole?'

'I most certainly do,' he said with vengeance. 'They have been wanting me to leave them alone ever since my ladies kept their meetings here.'

'I take it you mean temperance meetings?' Daniel asked.

'I certainly do . . . Why, it isn't right for grown men to go around plying themselves with strong liquor. Lawrence and I never drink.' He gave a little giggle, looked around and held his cheeks. 'Well, to be perfectly honest, we do take a naughty little sip of sherry on Christmas Day, but that's about all.'

Murphy cupped a massive hand around his mouth. 'We promise not to tell anyone,' he whispered.

70

'After breakfast we will make enquiries about the loss of your bunkhouse,' the marshal explained. 'I will ask the sheriff if he can shed any light on the subject.'

Jason waved his hands in the air. 'What! He's a dreadful man. No manners, no breeding and he smells like a dead polecat. Why they made him sheriff, I'll never know.'

Daniel rolled his eyes. 'I think we may have to have a word with Sheriff Sumner purely out of protocol, but before that may we have three breakfasts?'

'You may,' he replied as he flicked his head to one side. 'That's tea or coffee with flapjacks, and I wish you the very best of luck when you meet that onerous man.'

After breakfast, the marshal and his deputies walked to the sheriff's office and knocked on the door. After quite a while, and through the glass panel, a dirty white curtain moved slightly aside. 'My name is Marshal Wheetman. May we have a word?'

'What about?' an aged cry came from within.

'Nothing in particular; you see, we are here in town and need your help.'

Outside, they could hear two bolts being drawn, a key turning slowly, until eventually the door opened slightly. 'Show me your hands.' The sound of a crackled old voice came through the gap. 'Hurry now, I've got a gun.'

Daniel gave the other two a nod of compliance. 'We are officers of the law and want nothing more

71

than to have a chat.'

The door opened more fully and two barrels of a shotgun could be seen in the shaft of light coming from outside. The barrels moved from left to right as the sheriff told them to come in. Inside the stench of rotting flesh made their eyes water as the gloom of his office made it impossible to walk safely. 'My God, man,' the marshal blurted out. 'How can you live like this?' he said as he moved to open some drapes.

'Don't do that, sonny!' the sheriff shouted, pointing both barrels at Daniel.

With lightning speed Carver snatched the sheriff's gun away. 'You see, old-timer, you have to cock both hammers before this'll work. Go ahead, Marshal, open those drapes.'

In the increasing light they began to understand a little of how the sheriff had been living. In the centre of the room there was a broken stove, so old it would crumble to dust if anyone should touch it. Scattered everywhere were empty bottles and tins, boxes, blankets, old clothes and plenty of gone-off food, all playing home and host to do dozens of healthy and eager flies. Daniel took a handkerchief and covered his mouth as he wrenched open two small windows. 'This is despicable,' he gasped as a tiny amount of fresh air entered his nostrils.

Carver threw open the front door as Murphy did the same with the back. 'This ought to help, Marshal,' they both shouted.

The sheriff sank down in a corner to hide. 'Don't do it, boys, I beg of yer,' he cried.

'Don't do what?' Daniel asked.

'Don't tell the Kid where I am.'

'The Kid?' the marshal asked. 'What in the blazes are you talking about? What Kid?'

'The Kid . . . William Bonney, that's who,' his toothless mouth cackled back.

'William Bonney?' Daniel said with surprise.

Murphy spoke up as he opened the remaining windows. 'That's Billy the Kid, Marshal, also known as William Bonney. He hails from New Mexico.'

Daniel tutted. 'I know who William Bonney is . . . and, for your information, his real name is Henry McCarty, but for the life of me I can see no reason for this wretch to be in fear of him. Can you?'

Murphy rubbed his chin. 'Now you come to mention it, it don't make any sense.'

Carver broke open the barrels of the sheriff's shotgun and threw it on a table. ' 'Tain't even loaded,' he declared, and then his face lit up in surprise. 'Hey, I just thought, maybe Billy the Kid has sworn to kill the sheriff? By all accounts he done killed three already.'

Daniel pointed to the sheriff. 'Can you not see? This man is no sheriff. He was obviously placed here because of his degenerated state of mental health and not for his prize-winning ways of bringing criminals to justice.' The marshal pointed to a small portion of rotting deer carcass in the corner of the room. 'Would one of you wrap that up in a blanket and take it outside?' he asked. 'We will be sure to catch some obscure wild mountain disease if we allow

73

the stench to linger for a moment longer.'

'Not me, Marshal,' Murphy replied. 'I ain't doin' it.'

'Neither me either,' Carver added.

'Mister Handyside,' Daniel began. 'If we give you our word nothing will happen to you, may we ask if you would be so kind as to remove that object from this building immediately?'

Reluctantly, the sheriff crawled towards the offending item. 'This is all I gots to eat,' he said.

'Good heavens, man,' Daniel gasped. 'That thing has more life in it now than when it was happily bouncing through the fields. Just throw it away and we will provide you with more food than you will know what to do with.'

'All right . . . if you say so,' he grumbled.

'I do say so, and please take it out back rather than the front; we do not wish to offend passers-by.'

The sheriff grabbed the putrid remains, dragged it outside, hurried back to the safety of his office and took up a bullwhip.

'What ya thinking of doin' with that, old-timer?' Murphy asked.

'Flies,' he shouted back. 'Damn flies . . . They think I know somethin'. Some nights I hear 'em whisperin' behind my back.' He brandished the bullwhip for all to see. 'But I gets 'em with this.'

'This *hombre* is plumb loco,' Murphy commented.

'He is obviously suffering from some sort of paranoia, but that does not mean to say he is of no use to us.' He looked at the sheriff. 'I presume you are

Casper Handyside?'

'That's me, all right.'

'Mister Handyside, please stand up and come over to the light where we can see you better.'

Casper stood to his crooked full height of four feet nine and shuffled forward nervously. Before them stood a skeleton of a man with a long grey beard that mixed with his hair so well it was impossible to tell where one started and the other finished. His ragged lumber shirt was kept on his back by a worn out buckskin waistcoat, which was atop a pair of dusty bleached denim pants. His boots hardly had any more life in them; the soles flapped when he walked, which extenuated his pronounced limp. 'My poor man, how in the name of Hades did you get to be voted town sheriff?'

Casper tried to do a small jig but stumbled over in the process. 'There's plenty of life left in me yet.'

'There's more life in your clothes than I care to think about but one thing is certain: sheriff material you certainly are not. What did you do before they made you sheriff?'

'Shovelled horse shit.'

'Where?'

'Over at the livery.'

'And where did you live?'

'Over at the livery.'

'Permit me to be bold, but the way I understand things is that moving equine excrement from one spot to another is not one of the prime qualifications necessary to become a sheriff.'

'Hey?'

'Never mind. . . . Who voted you as sheriff?'

'Almost everyone. I told 'em I don't want the job but they just wouldn't listen. They got me fired an' I didn't have nowhere to live exceptin' this place.'

'That fixes it, Marshal,' Murphy interrupted. 'It's just like we was telling yer: they don't want no real law.'

'I am quite aware of that, Deputy,' Daniel turned and pointed to Casper. 'Why are you afraid of Billy the Kid?'

'The voice man told me.'

Daniel rolled his eyes. 'Well, I suppose it makes a change from talking flies. Mister Handyside, have you ever seen this man?'

Casper's eyes grew wide with fear. 'He lives in the shadows. I ain't never seen him but he speaks slow and clear like a ghost. He tells me what to do and he told me the Kid was gunnin' for me . . . I ain't been out of here for weeks.'

'Can you still hear him when you are in this office?'

'That's just it!' Casper said as he pointed across the street. 'I only hears him over yon, just next to that post ya see there.'

Daniel looked out across the street. 'Ah, very clever . . . I see how the whole trick is done.'

Murphy gazed in the same direction. 'See what, Marshal?'

'Never mind right now; I will explain some other time.' He turned to look at Casper. 'Mister

Handyside, have you any idea what goes on in this town?'

'What do ya mean, Marshal?'

'Who does what and to whom?'

'Ain't with yer, young fella.'

'I see your answer confirms what I already sus-pected to be the case.' He picked up a half empty bottle, which he suspected Casper had been drinking from and gave it a cautious sniff. 'Did you drink this?'

'Ain't nothing wrong with that, young fella; it ain't nothing but a health drink.'

Daniel passed the bottle Murphy who also gave it a sniff. 'Cactus juice: Marshal, this stuff sure sends you loco.'

'Peyote Cactus juice, if I am not mistaken; a very powerful hallucinogenic. With this, anyone could command this poor man's will, or anyone else's for that matter. Gentlemen, we are dealing with a very tricky customer, but first we must try to help Mister Handyside by getting him cleaned up and obtaining some new clothes as well as nourishing food – which, after all, is our Christian duty – but most important of all we must organise a work party to spruce up this jail.'

'Amen to that,' Carver agreed.

'Don't talk too soon,' Murphy huffed. 'Why do I get the feelin' we are about to be done up like some sort of sacrificial lambs?'

CHAPTER 7

Considering Casper's state of mental health, the marshal and his deputies thought it best to put the sheriff outside on a rocking chair until they had managed to clean up the jail. Daniel organised some brooms, buckets and mops and left Murphy and Carver to get on with the task whilst he took a look around the town.

It was midmorning and Cactus Ridge had fully woken up, so he decided to take a seat outside the general store and make a few notes.

He noticed there was an unusually high female population dashing here and there. The ladies outnumbered men almost twofold and most of the ladies were dressed in high fashion; there was hardly a farmer's wife to be seen. They gathered in small groups like wolves before the hunt, and he sensed they were all fragments of a larger group, waiting to assemble for a single purpose. As the morning began to move to midday, the groups of ladies got bigger and bigger until, with military precision, they filed

into two large lines about forty metres long. At the
spearhead were uniformed ladies, stoutly armed with
drums, tambourines and trumpets, who began to
play a marching song that spirited the army to mark
time. In the centre of the main street, a tall, slim lady
dressed in a dark green suit took position at the head
and gave a signal for the procession to begin. To the
tune of Let Us Pass This Goodly Measure, they
marched forward towards the Ace in the Hole
saloon.

Noticing one or two curious townsfolk were following the spectacle, the marshal used them as
camouflage and kept pace with the small army of
well-dressed ladies. With well-timed precision, every
fourth lady in each line took position like outriders
on a hunt; their job was to indiscriminately thrust
leaflets into the hands of anyone they should pass by,
regardless of age or gender.

A further total of six ladies went forth like skir-
mishers, hammering leaflets onto walls, barrels,
wagons and doors until, finally, they were forced to a
halt by nine well-armed cowboys that stood outside
the Ace in the Hole. A single man in a pinstriped suit
held up his right hand and addressed the ladies.
'Now, ladies,' he began, 'so far, there is no law that
states we cannot sell alcohol, and therefore I am
asking you, once again, to leave this town and return
to wherever you came from.'

The thin lady took a step forward. 'We are of the
temperance movement.' She turned to proudly waft
an arm at her army. 'We understand the evils of

drink: it is Satan's work and therefore we are on a mission from God.' From a black satin bag that hung over her left arm, she produced a bible and held it into the air. 'This is our cause, for it is written in the good book: "And be not drunken with wine, wherein is riot, but be filled with the spirit".'

The man gave a smile and a nod. 'Yes, yes, ladies, but as I keep on telling you there is no law that says I cannot sell wine nor strong drink, so you and yours–' he touched his black hat in respect '–Your lovely ladies have no right to stop folk from going about their lawful pursuits. Now, as owner of this saloon, I insist neither you or any one of your delegates enter this establishment for whatever reason.'

'Do you know who I am?' she asked indignantly.

'Nope,' he replied casually.

'I am Lady Clifton.'

The man gave a large smile. 'And do you know who I am?' he asked.

'Certainly not,' she replied.

'I'm the man who says you can't come in.'

Lady Clifton reared up like a duck about to fly. 'Come on, ladies, follow me,' she said out loud.

As the line began to move forwards it was stopped by the sound of nine repeating rifles loading bullets in their chambers.

'Now, ladies,' the man said as he turned his lapel to show a deputy sheriff's badge. 'As a duly appointed officer of the law, I am telling you all to disperse and let us go about our legitimate business. If you do not, we shall arrest you, Lady Clifton, and anyone else who does not comply to my order.'

'You do not frighten me, young man,' she answered calmly. 'For your information, I have fought gambling, prostitution and drunkenness, I have nursed Her Majesty's soldiers when wounded, treated those poor unfortunates with leprosy and fought the savages in Africa.'

The men pointed their rifles at the ladies. 'Now once again, I am telling you, you are not welcome in this saloon. Now go home before someone gets hurt.'

Lady Clifton gave a sigh, replaced the bible in her purse and turned around to address her passive army, 'Ladies, for my part, I fear no evil but many of you have husbands and children, so I cannot allow these men to take the opportunity to shoot you down whilst you are doing the Lord's work. As there is nothing illegal about standing outside this den of iniquity and trying to stop those poor men who have given in to temptation, that is precisely what we shall do.' She clapped her hands. 'Now come on, ladies, take your positions.' Like a well-oiled machine, the line disassembled and moved into four smaller groups, two directly outside the saloon and the other two blocking the street on both sides. 'Now,' she said with pride, 'let us see how many customers you receive today.'

The deputy gave instructions for each of his men to fire a single shot above the heads of Lady Clifton's army, which they did with expert ease, but the temperance ladies didn't flinch an inch. 'You see,' she began with Shakespearian drama, 'my ladies have no reason to fear Satan and his diabolical deeds.' She pointed skywards. 'The Lord is our shepherd; we shall not want.'

The gunmen each fired a second shot, hitting the ground directly in front of some ladies, but still they paid no attention as the band played on. Through the noise Murphy's and Carver's voices grew louder as they ran up the street. 'Marshal. . . . Marshal!' they shouted as they came running up close. 'What's all this gunfire?' Murphy growled.

Lady Clifton gave the command for the band to stop as Daniel stood up and showed his badge. 'Now let me fully appraise the situation,' he began. 'As I see it. . . .'

'Marshal!' the man in the pinstripe suit gasped. 'He's a marshal?'

Murphy moved up close and flicked the safety loop from his iron. Carver did the same. 'And who says he ain't?' he asked menacingly.

'Well . . . I mean, he doesn't look like a marshal.'

'Mister,' Murphy continued. 'I don't know who you are and I don't rightly care none neither, but I strongly suggest you take our word for it and tell your men to point their rifles to'rds the ground.' He fixed the suited man with an iron-like stare. 'Now!' he shouted.

After a few seconds the man smiled and patted one on the back. 'Do as he says, boys, and go inside and get yourselves a drink. I can handle this.' He looked at Daniel and held his hand out in friendship.

'James Wanamaker, Marshal. Pleased to make your acquaintance. I own this saloon.'

'Marshal Wheetman,' Daniel said as he gave a short bow. 'At your service sir.'

'Permit me to use a very tired cliché, Marshal. You ain't from around these parts, I take it?'

'Correct, Mister Wanamaker.'

'England?'

'Correct again, although I have spent some time in India.'

'Perhaps we could have a little chat inside my humble establishment?'

Overhearing their conversation, Lady Clifton gave a loud gasp and pointed to the Ace in the Hole. 'Look, ladies! Look how Satan gathers more souls and tempts those into that den of iniquity. Let us pray for their salvation.'

Daniel gave her a warm smile. 'Lady Clifton, I am well aware of your beliefs but I can assure you it is not my intention to allow alcohol to spoil my work, and I am certain you are more than welcome to join us for tea.' He looked at James, who gave an approving nod.

'Ladies!' she announced. 'It is for you that I do this; for you and God.'

Daniel moved to one side with great courtesy and removed his hat. 'After you, Lady Clifton.'

'Hmm!' she replied indignantly.

As they entered the saloon, all sound and movement ceased for a moment except when one or two cowboys removed their hats or shined their boots on the back of their trousers. James pulled out a chair for Lady Clifton to set herself down on and then joined both her and Daniel. 'Tea, my lady?' he asked.

'Tea will be fine, young man,' she answered graciously before placing her handbag on the table and folding her arms. 'I have been in many such establishments before, but this is somewhat cleaner. Not very clean, you understand, but a little cleaner.'

'Thank you, your Ladyship,' James replied as he beckoned the barkeep over. 'It is so nice to have such a distinguished guest.'

Like curious schoolchildren, Murphy and Carver came bursting though the door, their eyes scanning the trio. 'What do ya want us to do, Marshal?' Murphy shouted.

James looked up at Murphy and smiled. 'Ah, I see; like me, you are *locum tenens.*'

Murphy fixed him with a steely stare. 'Mister,' he retaliated. 'I ain't loco and you've got a big mouth which I'd love to shut.'

'*Lapsus linguae*, Deputy, a silly slip of the tongue; please forgive me.'

Daniel looked up impatiently. '*Locum tenens* means a deputy. . . . Until I inform you otherwise, consider us all to be incommunicado.'

Carver's eyes sparkled with a mischievous glint. 'Anythin' you say Marshal . . . Murphy and me, we'll go and see how the ruckus is goin' on outside.'

As they went outdoors, Carver turned to Murphy and with a puzzled look asked. 'Where in hell is

Communicardo? I've been to most places around theses parts and I ain't never heard of Communicardo.'

Murphy sucked a long deep breath through his teeth. 'Maybe it's near El Paso?'

'Wherever it is, the marshal sure ain't there.'

Murphy grinned just as a pretty young lady pushed a leaflet into his hand. 'Oh beggin' your pardon, miss,' he said as he removed his hat. 'I ain't one for reading and cipherin' much; you'd better have this back.'

'And what about your handsome friend?' she asked.

Carver began to blush. 'Aw, shucks, miss,' he replied. 'I ain't had much time to learn to read right good.'

She linked her arm in his and smiled. 'Then I will have to teach you myself,' she said as she led him away into the crowd of women.

'Carver!' Murphy shouted. 'What about the jail? I ain't doin it on my own.' But Carver could not hear. 'Well, don't that goddamn beat all?' he said as he turned to walk back down the street.

'Deputy?' a stout woman shouted.

'Yes, ma'am.'

'What is happening? Can we continue with our demonstration?'

'I reckon that's what the marshal and those other two are talking about right now, so if I was you I'd hang fire until they done come out.'

The stout lady looked puzzled as she looked down

the street. 'That's curious,' she mumbled. 'What is that infernal man shouting about?'

Murphy turned to see the tiny frame of Casper Handyside bouncing around with his arms flaying like a windmill in a hurricane. 'He's sure het up about somethin',' he said as the withered old sheriff ran towards them. 'What is it?' he yelled back.

Casper's gravel voice didn't travel well on the breeze as he shouted as hard as he could. 'It's the jail!'

Murphy cupped his ear with his hand. 'I think he's sayin' somethin' about the mail, but I ain't had no mail.'

'No, that isn't it, look!' she said. 'He's pointing above those buildings.'

'Pointing at what?'

'That cloud, I presume.'

As Casper got closer, Murphy's ears became accustomed to his frantic screams. 'The jail,' he yelled.

'What's wrong with the jail?' Murphy asked.

'It's on fire!'

CHAPTER 8

In the aftermath of the jail burning to the ground, the marshal met Murphy and Carver in the converted church known as the Baptist Tabernacle. In order to bring more brethren into the flock, the minister, Mathew Hickman, decided to turn the place into an eating house, offering food and drink at reasonable rates.

It was a single-storey building with a high ceiling held up by large wooden joists, from which hung several cartwheels, each holding ten candles around their rims. The floor was polished mahogany, matching the redwood tables and chairs that were placed around the room, each equidistant from the other. In the middle was a pump organ, at which sat an elderly lady dressed in puritan black and white, who rhythmically drove it with her feet as she pumped out a never-ending selection of hymns. This entertainment was regularly interrupted every hour by a short service whereby customers and staff gave praise to the Lord.

The food was simple, good and cheap, so despite having compulsory religion served with every meal it attracted as many as twenty townsfolk at any one time.

As the marshal and his deputies waited for their waitress, Daniel called them to task.

'Once more, the pair of you never cease to amaze,' he began. 'We have hardly been in this town twenty-four hours and you have managed to burn down two buildings. You must let me know the secret of your success.'

Carver dropped his head. 'We ain't got no secret, Marshal.'

Murphy leaned closer and whispered, 'Once agen, it weren't our fault.'

'Then pray tell me: whose fault was it?'

Murphy shuffled uneasily in his chair. 'Well, it sort of was our fault, but we didn't mean to burn the jail down. It just sort of happened.'

'Yeah, Marshal, it just happened,' Carver added.

Daniel leaned back in his chair and took his lapels in his hands. 'Please continue,' he said.

'Well, Carver and me was doin' just as you told us to. We was tryin' to get the place in good order when those flies kept on comin' back into the jail; we think they were lookin' for that rotten bit of deer we done throwed out. Anyway, Carver and me thought it best to have a little fire outside so as to burn the meat and kill the smell. We also thought we'd burn those rag tag drapes and one or two other things.' He looked at the marshal with sheepish eyes.

88

'Go on,' Daniel said quietly.

'Well, we got things goin' pretty good: the fire was a burnin' and we kept good watch on the sparks that came from the wood we used, when all of a sudden we heard gunshots comin' from up the street. We thought you was in terrible trouble so we ran to help. How was we to know the fire would spread?'

The marshal leaned forwards, clenched his hands, placed his arms on the table and gave a short sigh. 'I suppose accidents will happen, but why are the both of you always in the centre of things?'

'It was just as Murphy said, Marshal. We got distracted by the sound of gunshots, and as deputies,' he placed his hand on his heart, 'duly sworn to do our duty, we had to come to your help, Marshal.'

Daniel took a moment or two to consider their pleas. 'Very well, we will speak no more of it, but if you continue to reduce the amount of buildings in Cactus Ridge at the rate you are, by winter there will be nothing left but a pile of smouldering pieces of timber.'

'We won't do nothin' like it agen, Marshal,' Murphy pledged. 'You got our words on that.'

'I fear those words will echo in my head for years to come.'

Murphy began to smile. 'Anyway, Marshal, what did that Lady Whatshername and the fella in the fancy suit have to say?'

'Lady Clifton is, as you may have gathered, part of a temperance movement who feel they have a mission to stop the consumption of alcohol, and

James Wanamaker is not sympathetic to their cause. However, he is quite within his rights not to allow any temperance movement ladies into his establishment, and therefore is not breaking any laws in doing so.

'On the other hand, Lady Clifton has every right to lead her ladies in peaceful protest, just as long as they stay within the confines of the law, and I have merely informed them of their rights.'

Carver's ears pricked up. 'So does that mean Bathsheba ain't goin' to be arrested, Marshal?'

'Bathsheba? Who in the name of all that is holy is Bathsheba?' the marshal asked.

Carver rolled the corners of his hat in his hands nervously as his face went red with embarrassment. 'We just met today. She sure is pretty and smells real sweet too. . . . She's goin' to teach me to read like a schoolteacher does.'

Murphy began to laugh. 'You mean that little lady I saw ya goin' off with is a schoolteacher?'

'Damn right she is,' Carver nodded. 'And she's real good at reading and cipherin'. I even bet she could out-read you, Marshal.'

Daniel leaned back and took up his lapels once again. 'Am I to believe you are taking reading lessons from a lady who is involved with the temperance movement?'

'You can bet your bottom dollar, Marshal.'

'Are you thinkin' of sparkin' with her?' Murphy asked.

'What I thinks and what you knows are two separate things.'

' 'Tain't too. As your partner I needs to know.'

'Don't neither.'

'Children, children. . . . Once again you are behaving like schoolchildren,' the marshal interrupted.

'He started it,' Murphy protested.

'Did not,' Carver replied.

Daniel held his hands to his ears. 'Stop it, stop it,' he said sharply. 'Will the pair of you please stick to matters in hand?'

'I will if he will,' Carver insisted as he stubbed his finger on the table.

'I sure will, but I ain't the one goin' to marry a woman who hates a man like me to have the occasional drink now and agen.'

Daniel sat forwards and stared at them both. 'Not another word!' he snapped. 'From now on and until we leave this establishment I do not wish to hear either of you uttering the slightest sound. Understood?'

They both nodded their heads in agreement as an ageing puritan waitress approached their table. 'May the Lord be with you,' she said with a sweet smile.

'And with you, sister,' Daniel replied.

'What can I get you, boys?' she asked.

'What do you recommend?'

'Stew is good,' she replied.

'Do you have anything else?' he asked.

'Apple pie, tea or coffee.'

Daniel cleared his throat and gave a slight grin. 'In that case, may I have tea, stew and apple pie three times please?'

91

'Twenty minutes,' she said as she turned to walk away.

After a few minutes silence Murphy could stand it no more. 'Marshal?' he said. 'We've been thinkin' . . . We ain't got the bunkhouse to sleep in an' we ain't got the jail neither, so could we sleep in that fancy caravan of yours?'

The marshal's eyes grew wide with disbelief. 'Do my ears deceive me?' He leaned closer and began to whisper. 'The only reason you cannot sleep in the bunkhouse is because you two pyromaniacs burned it to the ground. You did the same with the jail, and now you wish to add my caravan to your list of achievements. The only place left is the livery stable and, considering the amount of loose combustible material there is to be found there, I hold very little hope for its future.'

'Does that mean no?' Murphy asked.

'It most certainly does,' he said as he took to his feet. 'And whilst I am away using the bathroom, please try to behave yourselves.'

'Sure will, Marshal,' they both said.

Soon after they were alone Carver took the chance to ask Murphy about the Little Bighorn.

'You never have said much about Little Bighorn. Any reason?' he asked.

Murphy gave a tired sigh and lit his cheroot. 'Ain't much to tell,' he replied.

'Maybe, but how come you got mixed up in it all?'

'I was in my twenties when it happened. Custer had been chasin' the Sioux for weeks. I hated the man for all he'd done to my friends and family, not to mention thousands of other Indians. He was so full of himself, wantin' to be a brigadier general again, maybe even president, but there was nothing in his heart except ambition and he cared for nothing but himself.

'I'd finished scoutin' for him years before. He said I was a deserter but that ain't true. I told him from the outset I was only goin' to be with him for a year or so, but when I saw some of the terrible things he'd done, I had had my belly full of George Armstrong Custer and I left.

'He came upon me when I was punchin' cattle in Colorado; he'd been spending most of his time fightin' with the Cheyene. I didn't think he'd remember me, but he did and had me arrested. All the time he travelled north into Montana I was tied up like a hog and tortured. He said it was an example to his men not to disobey his orders. I could see it in his eyes he was crazy, even then.

'Well, had it not been for Klondike he'd have killed me for sure, but I snook away in the night and kept on runnin' . . . I swear I could hear old Yellow Hair scream five miles away when he found out I'd gone.

'Anyway, I was sure in a bad way: no food, no water, no horse . . . I was just about done for when a huntin' party of Sioux Indians found me and took me in. Sitting Bull himself was leading them; like me, he was a young buck but he also was a powerful medicine man even then and he said my spirit was clean and good.

'For a while I settled down with them and met Dancing Bird, me and her hit it off straight away and ... well ... you know the rest.' He threw his cheroot onto the floor, ground it out with his boot and dropped his head for a few seconds. 'Anyway, after I'd left I worked here and there, even robbin' a bank or two until, one day, I saw Custer agen. He was ridin' at the front, all high and mighty, whilst some of his men played Garryowen on their tin whistles.

'Right then and there I decided to follow 'em and kill the son of a bitch first chance I got. At the beginnin' I didn't give two hoots what would happen to me if I got caught – all I wanted to do was kill him – but then I followed him for weeks and changed my mind. I still wanted him dead, all right, but I wasn't goin' to hang for it.

'I'd learned real good how to survive on my own: what to eat, how to lay animal traps. . . . Oh, sure, I knew some stuff before, but those Indian friends of mine showed me more than I had ever dreamed of.

'From the high ground I watched as Custer drove those boys of his without rest. His lust for glory had taken his mind and he wasn't thinking straight. He was hard on the trail of the Sioux and the northern Cheyenne; the tracks left by the Indians were sometimes two hundred yards wide. I don't know how many there were but it was clear from the tracks he was not dealin' with a small tribe: this was almost the entire Sioux nation and the Dakota tribe.

'Custer must have thought a victory over the entire nation would have set him in the history books for

good and he must have denied advice from his officers to take cannon and such because he wanted to
go as fast as he could after the Indians. To make
matters worse, Crazy Horse had attacked General
George Crook's force with over a thousand men two
months earlier and delayed Crook joinin' Custer's
troop, but instead of waitin', the fool went right on
ahead and chased after the Indians.

'As Custer got close to the Sioux and Cheyenne I
rode on ahead and warned 'em he was close, but they
already knew: the goddamned fool had made a dust
trail a blind man could follow – not only did he have
flags, banners and such, but he kept those men
playin' his favourite song for most of the time.

'So he could get all the glory, he split his troops
and the madman attacked with half his cavalry. He
must have thought he was attackin' a small Indian
village; it was something he'd done so many times so
I guess he didn't think he'd have a battle on his
hands. He'd always thought the Indians were cow-
ardly, backward savages and his plan, like always, was
to capture the women and children, kill a few, and
the men would surrender . . . but not this day. This
day was to be his last.

'As soon as Custer realised what was goin' on, he
ordered his men to dismount and slaughter as many
Indians as possible with an "impenetrable line of
fire", as he called it. It was suicide right from the
start, but he thought his men would kill enough
bucks so the rest would loose heart and stop the
attack. The trouble was, Sitting Bull and his braves

were riled up something terrible and there was no way they was goin' to let Custer go. They had Yellow Hair right where they wanted him and they took their time about it; during the battle some warriors even rode back to camp, grabbed something to eat or drink and rode off to battle shoutin' 'This is a good day to die'.

'The rest of Custer's troops were pinned down somewhere else; Reno was in charge and he wasn't what Crazy Horse, Sitting Bull and Chief Gall wanted. They could have massacred his men too, but it was Custer they was after.

'Sitting Bull himself watched from the top of a hill and he saw what the five battalions of the 7th was doin' and he realised they was havin' trouble returnin' fire. Most of the men were spending time tryin' to get their rifle to work; I saw it myself.

'You see, they was armed with a Springfield trap-door rifle that kept on jammin' . . . I reckon it was because Custer had made his men ride so hard and for so long those copper cartridge cases had gone green and the men couldn't get 'em out after they'd been fired; they sort of swelled up with the heat or somethin'. During the battle some of the men prised the spent shells out with a knife, some used wood to push them out, some almost broke their teeth and fingers tryin' but it was no use: they couldn't fire more than a shot every now and agen.

'Sitting Bull had had a vision they would have a great victory and, spurred on by this, some of his warriors began to ride through Custer's men slashin' with their knives. The soldiers didn't have no swords to fight back with because Custer ordered they not take 'em. Soon the troopers were too panicked to do very much except wait to die. I even heard one or two shout for help from their mom; it was a sorry sight.

'I was watchin' what was goin' on from a hill. With me was sixty or so warriors cutting down Custer's men from afar; they was pickin' 'em off like rats in a barrel. I counted they had seven Henry rifles, ten Winchesters, nine Springfields, muzzle loaders from the war, army and navy Colts . . . Two of 'em had buffalo guns and suchlike, so all they had to do was keep on firin' and that would have been the end of Custer and his men, but those other braves who was doin' the attackin' wanted to make a slow killin', so they toyed with Custer and those poor boys of his.

'I know I didn't kill any of the 7th but I didn't try to stop Sitting Bull and Crazy Horse neither.

'After I saw the yellow-haired bastard drop to the ground, my rage went, I rode away, left Montana and came back south.'

Carver remained silent for a few moments, surreptitiously produced his hip flask and took a drink. 'To the South,' he said.

'To the South,' Murphy replied.

CHAPTER 9

The following morning Murphy and Carver woke up to the sound of a marching band going down the street. Carver looked out of the loft and saw Bathsheba right in the middle of the procession. 'Bathsheba!' he shouted as he waved. 'We're up here, Murphy and me.'

Bathsheba turned, looked up and waved back. 'She sure is pretty,' Carver said whilst grinning from ear to ear. 'And smart too.'

'Now, Carver, take my advice and don't get sweet on her; she's agen drinkin' and everythin'.'

'I knows that,' he grumbled back. 'She's just helping me with readin' and such.'

'Well it don't look like it to me. Besides, we're here to do as the marshal tells us and he's not goin' to tell us to go walkin' out with no townsfolk, that's for sure.' He picked up his hat, dusted some straw from his britches and headed for the ladder. 'Come on now, let's go and see what the marshal wants us to do next.'

98

As they were headed for the Last Trading Post they saw the marshal appear through the front door. 'Good morning, Deputies,' he said out loud. 'May I have a word?'

'Sure thing, Marshal,' Murphy agreed.

As they came close, Daniel looked at Carver. 'From what I deduce you have formed a relationship with a young lady from the temperance movement?'

Carver's eyes grew wide. 'I ain't neglectin' my official duties, Marshal. She's just helping me with reading and such.'

'No, no, that's very good,' Daniel replied. 'I want you to continue with those lessons; maybe she might say something interesting. Who knows?'

Carver grinned at Murphy. 'Haw, haw,' he said. 'The marshal wants me to stick close to Bathsheba.'

'That don't mean you have to spark her.'

'I ain't doin' nothing of the sort, I is doin' reading.'

'And you, Murphy,' Daniel said as he handed him ten dollars, 'I want you to sober up Mister Handyside, get him some new clothes and bring him to me around three o'clock. I shall be at the Baptist Tabernacle.'

'But he's been drinkin' cactus juice. How do I sober him up?'

Daniel passed him a small glass vial containing a golden liquid. 'Make certain he drinks this.'

Murphy looked at it with distrust. 'What's in it, Marshal?'

'An antidote.'

'Will it work?'

'Indeed it will. You see, Mister Handyside has been given the juice from the peyote cactus, and the adverse chemical it contains produces symptoms such as paranoia and schizophrenia.'

'What's this paranoia do to ya, Marshal?'

'Paranoia? Erm, it is the feeling that someone or something is against you, or about to harm you, or animals conspire to affect your doom, that sort of thing.'

'And the other word you used . . . skit something?'

'Schizophrenia? Well, very often, one symptom accompanies the other; the person suffering from this problem may hear voices, or receive visions from God, even instructions from the Devil. It is quite complicated, but Mister Handyside is clearly suffering from paranoid schizophrenia.'

'How do I get him to take it, Marshal?'

'Use your imagination, Deputy, but most of all be kind and gentle. You may have to coax him or trick him. Either way, the sooner he takes it the sooner he will begin to become more lucid.'

'Why do we want Old Casper anyroads? He's just an old fool.'

'If that is what you believe, others believe it also, and Old Casper, as you call him, may be able to tell us a great deal more than we think.'

'Where is the old fool now?'

'Well, seeing as how you managed to make the poor man homeless, I felt it necessary to tilt matters in his favour a little, so I paid for him to sleep in a storeroom in this very hotel.'

Murphy's face went red as his anger took over. 'You mean to say Carver and me has had to sleep in a hay loft whilst Old Casper has been in this hotel?'

'Only overnight, and only in the broom cupboard. You will find him if you go through a small red door on your far left. I doubt if he is awake, so please be gentle with him, and I shall meet you both at three p.m.'

Murphy was in no mood for any of this as he looked at the vial, so he shrugged his shoulders, entered the hotel, walked across to the red door, opened it, saw Casper on the floor, grabbed his nose, opened his mouth and poured the liquid down his throat. 'That ought to do it,' he said with a satisfied nod. 'Kind and gentle never fails.'

Casper's eyes opened wider than ever before as he grabbed his throat and tried to speak. 'Whaaa!' he said in a painful wheeze. 'Whaaa, whaaa, whaaa . . . what the hell was that?'

'Bath time,' Murphy said as he grabbed Casper by one arm and threw him over his shoulder like he was an old sack. He strolled casually, carrying the wriggling skeleton of a man to a horse trough, and threw him in. 'That ought to do too,' he said as the water-spluttering Casper struggled to get out.

'Now listen here, old-timer: here's five dollars. Now get over to the store and buy some duds, then get a haircut and meet me at the Ace in the Hole. Got that?'

Despite still being under the influence of the

cactus juice, Casper saw in Murphy's eyes he was in no mood to be trifled with. 'Yes, sir!' he replied. 'Errr, straight away, sir. Doin' it now, sir.'

In a temper, Murphy kicked a stone on the ground then held out his hand. 'And give me that tin star; you ain't no sheriff no more.'

Casper's trembling hand undid his badge. 'Anythin' you say, sir. You're the boss.'

Murphy gave Casper a helping hand in the form of his boot behind his backside. 'Now get, and do as I tell yer.'

Casper scurried across the street towards the general store, leaving a trail of water behind him as Murphy took a deep breath. 'Do this, do that,' he mumbled. 'You two can sleep in the bunkhouse, you two sleep under my caravan, I swear if'n the marshal gets killed in the next two years it'll be me what's done the killin'.' He mumbled and chuffed all the way to the saloon and as he flung the doors open he grumbled some more.

'Ah, good morning, Deputy.' A voice from a table in the far corner echoed through the empty building. 'How is the marshal today?'

'Friend, he's the most contrary son of a bitch I ever did know, and I've known a few.'

'James Wanamaker's the name. It's a little early for a drink, don't you think? Why not join me in coffee, pancakes and syrup? There's far too much for me. Besides, I would welcome your company.'

Murphy smiled. 'That's mighty neighbourly of ya, don't mind if I do.'

From under the table James pushed a chair out with his feet. 'Sit down, my friend,' he said as he snapped his fingers.

'Yes, sir?' A voice came from behind the bar.

'Roger, please bring another cup, plate and fork for our guest.'

'Sure thing, Mister Wanamaker.'

Murphy sat down, took off his hat, placed it on the table and reached across for a friendly handshake. 'Murphy's the name,' he said with a smile.

'Pleased to meet you, Murphy ... The marshal speaks very highly of you. He tells me you used to work at the Star Diamond in Crows Creek?'

'Sure did. Made a mighty good job of it too, even though I do say so myself.'

James Wanamaker gave out a loud laugh. 'I like that in a man: pride in his work.' The barkeep placed an extra cup on the table, which the landlord began to fill with coffee. 'Please, help yourself to pancakes. Have as many as you want.'

Almost before he's finished his words, Murphy grabbed three with his fork and smothered them with syrup. 'These are mighty fine pancakes, Mister Wanamaker,' he said as he filled his mouth almost to bulging.

'Please call me James.' He tipped back in his chair and lit a cigar with a satisfied air. 'My barman, Roger, told me how you and your friend handled yourselves the other night when three cowboys tried to get you both to lose your tempers. I owe you a debt of gratitude.'

103

'Just a few boys letting off steam, that's all.'

'Most commendable. I could use a couple of men like you.'

Murphy rubbed his chin. 'I'll bear that in mind, but we has to stick with the marshal . . . It's complicated.'

'That is a shame . . . I hear Moses Carver is fast with a gun.'

'I reckon so,' Murphy agreed. 'Me and Carver ain't been together very long, but I've seen enough.'

'Yesterday you both got nine of my men to stand down. It would appear your reputation doth precede you, my friend.'

Murphy shovelled more pancakes into his mouth and chewed them ravenously before giving a bulbous swallow. 'Nine men?' he said. 'Sure is a lot of men for saloon guards. . . .'

James grinned. 'You're fishing, Mister Murphy. I also like that in a man but the truth is no secret: I have a twenty thousand acre spread a few miles north of here. It is called the Gilded Lilly; rather an odd name for a ranch, don't you think?'

Murphy shrugged his shoulders. 'Don't bother me none,' he replied. 'What does interest me is why ain't you there lookin' after things and that?'

'Just one of my business interests. I have a finger in many pies, you may say.'

'The woman that was killed, did you know her?' Murphy asked.

'But of course: she was Lady Clifton's predecessor, a lady called Asquith. Her uncle is a man of some substance in Chicago.'

'And why was she killed?'

'The reason she was shot is for the marshal to dis-
cover, but we all have our suspicions.'

'And yours is?'

'My suspicions are my business and mine alone. It
is the facts that count and in this case there are very
few other than she lead the temperance movement
and she was shot.'

'Were you in town when it happened, Mister . . .
Er, James?'

'As a matter of fact, I was not: I was on a business
trip some seventy miles away, and when I returned
and found out what had happened I was shocked to
say the least.'

Murphy used his fork to cut the last of his pancakes like a surgeon uses a scalpel. 'You sure are a
busy man, Mister Wan . . . Er, James.'

'Indeed I am,' he said as he rose to his feet. 'And
now if you would forgive me, I have an appointment
in my office across the street, but please help yourself
to another coffee. If you could manage some more
pancakes, just ask Roger; he'll be only too happy too
oblige.'

Murphy looked out of the window across the
street. 'There's an iron shop and another place with
fancy curtains,' he said.

The landlord glanced sideways. 'The office with
the "fancy curtains" is where I practice law. I am an
attorney.'

'You?' Murphy gasped. 'You're a lawyer?'

105

'For my sins,' he replied. 'I presume the marshal has not had the time to inform you, or maybe it slipped his mind.'

Murphy grinned as he waved his greasy fork in James' direction. 'Not Marshal Wheetman, nothing slips his mind. He's the cleverest man I have ever met. He can work out who did what and when. He even can tell yer who's touched stuff and that.' He shook his head in pride. 'I'm telling yer, if the marshal is on your trail you're a dead man, that's for sure.'

James straightened his pinstripe suit. 'I will have to bear that in mind, Deputy. Good day.'

'Yes,' Murphy replied. 'And thanks for the pancakes and coffee.' He finished his breakfast, stood up and went over to the bar.

'What'll it be, sir?' the barkeep asked.

'Nothin', just to say thanks, that's all, and to ask about the woman that was shot. Did you know her?'

'Yes, she often came into this saloon. The boss and her would sit together for hours.'

'Honestly?' Murphy gasped.

'Oh, yes . . . I think she may have been preaching to him about the evils of drink. Either way she was never the type to cause problems, she was rather sweet.'

'Then how did all this ruckus that we saw yesterday begin?'

'Well, it did start before she was shot, but if anything she tried to stop it. Her methods were more gentle.'

'Could it have been an accident?'

'Not at all, she was shot in her room.'

'Where at?'

'The Last Trading Post, at the end of the street.'

'Much obliged,' he said as he replaced his hat. 'You've bin mighty helpful.'

'No trouble.'

Murphy went back into the street to find the marshal and tell him what he had found out but he ran into twenty or so women carrying placards and bouncing to the rhythm of the drums. 'This man has sinned,' one of them shouted, pointing to Murphy. 'The evils of drink have taken his soul; let us pray for his deliverance from Satan.'

'Amen to that!' a man shouted.

Murphy stopped and looked at the crowd. 'Carver?' he shouted in disbelief. 'What the hell are you doin'? You ain't teetotal and you know it.'

Carver grinned. 'I seen the light, Deputy.'

'Don't you "Deputy" me nothin', you just get back here . . . I've got some news for the marshal.'

'And I've got some news for you: Casper is over yon and it looks like he's about to hightail it.'

'How's he gonna do that without a horse?'

'Looks like he don't need one; he's saddling up Sea Biscuit.'

'What!' Murphy screamed as he ran towards the livery stable. 'Casper, you son of a bitch, I'll skin you alive!'

As he got to the door, his giant shadow projected in front of Old Casper. 'What do ya think you're up

107

to?' He growled.

'He'll kill me if I don't get away,' Casper pleaded. 'The Kid will kill me.'

'I'll kill ya if'n ya do, you crazy old man.'

Casper fell to the ground and began to cry. 'This isn't what I want,' he sobbed. 'All I wanted was peace and quiet . . . maybe the odd smoke and a glass or two of sippin' whiskey. Ain't that too much to ask for an old man who fought for the south?'

'Then why did you become sheriff?'

'I had no choice; all the folks around here told me I had no choice, otherwise they'd tell the Kid I was 'ere. I was frightened . . . and now YOU'RE gonna kill me.'

Murphy gave a sigh, lifted the old man up, placed him on a bale of hay and gave him a cheroot. 'No . . . I ain't goin' to kill ya.' He gave Casper a smile. 'If'n I did I reckon the marshal would have my guts for garters.' He grabbed Casper gently by the back of his neck. 'Come on, old-timer. It's time someone was nice. I'll buy you some breakfast.'

'The Kid won't be there, will he?' Casper asked.

Murphy gave him a comforting smile and put his hand on his shoulder. 'No, old-timer, the Kid won't be there.'

CHAPTER 10

Three o'clock arrived and the marshal awaited Murphy in the Baptist Tabernacle. As he watched the other customers he took notes about their code of dress, what they were eating, how they sat and with whom they socialised. To Daniel, the whole thing was a rich storehouse of information that he could not ignore.

In the centre of the room a grey-haired old lady played 'Amazing Grace' softly on the pump organ. She had the Olney Hymns book in front of her and, from the position her current song was in the order of play, it looked like she had been there for two hours and was planning to be there for another two.

Her voice was quiet, calm and serene and the twenty or so other diners listened to her songs with obvious delight. The whole atmosphere was one of a holy calm, church-like and pure. In the corner was a very small log fire that burned completely unnecessarily other than to placate a ginger cat that was lying in the pool of gentle heat that radiated forth.

This was the scene when the door burst open suddenly with Murphy reversing through it. Previously he'd picked up several stones and was hurling them at an object that only he was aware of. 'Now listen to me, you crazy old fool: when I tells ya not to goddamn follow me anymore, I don't want ya to goddamn follow me,' Murphy shouted out loud. 'Now go on and git, before I shove my boot up your arse.'

Snatching his hat off, he threw it to the floor in anger as he stared at Daniel. 'Marshal, that crazy old man keeps stickin' to me like a shadow. I ain't been able to go nowhere without him.' His eyes took on a mischievous look as he pointed to the marshal and grinned. 'Can I shoot the crazy son of a bitch? I promise the little runt would be dead before you could count up to two.'

The music stopped and the only sound that could be heard was from the cat, which gently purred as it snoozed, completely undisturbed by Murphy's arrival.

The horrified deputy looked around, slowly picked up his hat and twisted the brim in his massive hands. 'Errr . . . Sorry folks for all that swearin' and cussin', but there's a man out there that follows me like he was a puppy dog, I ain't got no chance to have a slash . . . I mean take a piss . . . er, sorry . . . answer the call of nature without him standin' right next to me. He was even rubbing up agen me, and I don't knows about all of you but I ain't able to go when someone is standin' there a-watchin' me.'

110

The grey-haired lady stood up slowly from the organ, walked towards him and took his arm gently. 'Come, my child, we are all friends here,' she said as Casper opened the door a little. 'Is this your friend?' she asked calmly.

Murphy's eyes grew wide as his nostrils flared. 'He ain't no friend of mine,' he blurted out. 'Look! He's comin' right after me just like I said he would, and like a puppy dog too.'

Casper entered the Tabernacle on all fours, his grey beard tangled in the dust on the floor as he whimpered for attention. 'Oh, dear,' the surprised old lady said. 'I do think we may have a slight problem.'

'Slight problem?' Murphy gasped. 'This old man thinks he's a goddamned dog, beggin' your pardon agen, ma'am, er . . . folks.'

The puritanical lady gave a gentle smile and patted Casper on the head. 'Maybe we should humour him for a little while?' she asked.

Murphy's face went red with rage. 'And I suppose we should throw him a stick, or give him a bone, or let him have a cosy place near the fire, next to that mangy cat over yon.'

As Casper's head turned to look at the cat, he began to growl and slowly stalk the sleeping creature. 'Do something, Marshal,' Murphy shouted. 'Before there's merry hell.'

Daniel gave a whistle, patted the chair next to him and beckoned for Casper to come. Without delay his command was followed, and the ex-sheriff sat next to the marshal, panting as he did so. 'Deputy, I take it you followed my instructions?'

'About what, Marshal?'

'You gave Mister Handyside the antidote in a kind and gentle manner?'

Murphy gave a naughty grin. 'Sure did, Marshal, I was as gentle as a lamb.'

'Then why, pray say, is he suffering from delirium tremens?'

'Deal rum what?' he snapped back.

Daniel took to his feet and pointed at the dog form Casper. 'Because you failed to adhere to my strict instructions, we now have a case of mental morphing on our hands. How long he will continue to believe he is some sort of canine I do not know, but what I do know is you will have to keep good care of him until he becomes *compos mentis* once again, should such a state of homeostasis ever be achieved.'

Murphy scratched his head in thought. 'Does what you just said mean what I think it means?'

The marshal gave a long sigh and then cocked his head to listen to a squawking sound, which was getting louder. 'What is that infernal noise?' he asked as Casper started to growl.

'Sounds like somebody's tryin' to stuff a chicken without killin' it first,' Murphy replied.

The sound got louder until it stopped outside the door. Everyone held their breath as the door handle turned slowly, allowing the door to swing open and reveal Carver standing there, grinning proudly with a bugle in his hand. 'Howdy, folks,' he said with enthusiasm. 'How do ya like my bugle playin'? Kinda good, don't ya think?'

'Deputy, how can I put this?' the marshal began. 'I have been to numerous recitals, many operas, dozens of concerts and several musicals and I feel it fair to inform you I have never witnessed music such as the caterwaul you have just manufactured.'

Carver's face lit up with delight. 'Why, thank ya, Marshal, that's mighty friendly of ya to say that . . . What about you, Murphy? What do you make of it?'

'Give us another blast on that there thing,' he asked enthusiastically.

'Sure will.' Carver blew his horn once more to the howling accompaniment of Casper. 'What in hell's bells is he howlin' at? Sounds like a lovesick coyote to me.'

Murphy grinned a stupid grin. 'He thinks he's a dog. The marshal says it's somethin' to do with comin' off drinkin' that cactus juice.'

Daniel gave another sigh. 'What he is trying to explain so badly is Mister Handyside has, for some time now, been drinking a hallucinogenic substance that has many side effects whilst under its influence. The most common is paranoid schizophrenia, and there is some reason why he has been given this toxic potion in the first place. What we are trying to do is bring him back to normality in a controlled manner, but thanks to your fellow deputy it would appear he has slipped into this terrible state of delirium.'

Carver looked around to see who was listening.

'We're still in the state of Texas, Marshal,' he whispered.

'What?' Daniel gasped.

'Texas State . . . I'm tryin' to tell yer, Marshal, we're ain't in no state of delirium, and I can't rightly say I ever heard of it, neither – and I've bin almost everywhere. I've bin to New Mexico, Kansas, Arizona, Montana, Arkansas, California . . Wichita. . . '

'Hey, I've bin to Wichita,' Murphy interrupted. 'Met a girl there, six feet seven she was and as slim as a match. In fact she looked a little like a Lucifer, her skin bein' so pale and all underneath that lock of bright red hair, but she sure was pretty.'

'What was her name?' Carver asked.

Murphy rubbed his chin. 'Millie . . . no, Mollie . . . or was it Maggie?'

'Deputies, may we attend to the matter at hand, which at this moment is Mister Handyside?' Daniel pleaded.

'Sure thing, Marshal,' Murphy agreed. 'What do ya want me to do with him?'

'Despite your protestations it is necessary for you to take him with you wherever you go.'

'Aw, shucks, Marshal! He's drivin' me crazy. Would it be alright if'n I tie him up over at the livery stable and feed him now and then?'

'Now listen to me, Deputy: despite the fact he is behaving like a dog, and to a degree smells rather like a dog, there is no reason to treat him like a dog.'

'Well what was all that whistlin' and pattin' the chair all about if you weren't treatin' him like a dog?'

'That was necessary, but to tie him up and leave him over at the livery stable certainly is not.'

'Give him to Carver, Marshal. Please, I'm beggin' yer. I've had my belly full.'

'Oh, very well,' Daniel agreed. 'Carver, take Mister Handyside and look after him until he stops believing he is a dog.'

'Can I practise my bugle, Marshal?'

'Oh, very well, but do it somewhere else.'

'Where, Marshal?'

'Anywhere at all, just so long as it is out of earshot.'

'I gotchya,' he grinned. 'I need to be real good for the Sunday precession.'

'What precession?' Murphy asked.

'The Temperance League is havin' a march on Sunday and I get to march with 'em playin' this 'ere bugle.'

'You're with 'em?' Murphy screamed.

'Sure am. From now on it's the straight and narrow for me. I ain't goin' to touch the devil's brew no more.'

'Never?'

'Never. Cross my heart and spit on the floor.'

Murphy replaced his hat and went to sit down. 'If that don't beat all,' he mumbled. 'Moses Carver never takin' a sip of whiskey no more . . . That ain't right.'

Carver strode up to Casper, grabbed the back of his belt and carried him out like he was a suitcase. 'You're comin' with me, old-timer. You can listen to me doin' a little practising on this here bugle whilst you get sober.'

The marshal took a deep breath, sat next to Murphy and addressed the others in the room. 'Ladies and gentlemen, please forgive the casual manner with which my deputies conduct themselves. I can assure you it will never happen again.'

As if nothing had happened, the grey-haired lady began to pump and sing once more as Murphy leaned closer to the marshal. 'Marshal, I found out something real interestin',' he whispered. 'That pilgrim who owns the saloon is a lawyer and he also owns a spread north of here.'

Daniel took a casual sip of tea. 'I already know that,' he replied. 'His name is above the door of his office and the fact he has a ranch is common knowledge.'

'That ain't all: he kept company of the woman who was shot.'

'I also know this.'

'Well what you don't know is she had a boss in Chicago, a city fella who has some sort of business.'

'What are you trying to tell me, Deputy? I already know this as well.'

'Aw, shucks, Marshal, ain't there nothin' you don't know?'

'I don't know who shot Miss Asquith, or why she was shot, but I have my suspicions and it is possible Mister Handyside may be able to help.'

Murphy gasped. 'That old fool? Why, he's crazier than a barrel of frogs.'

'He may appear to be crazy, as you call it, but I

believe that somewhere in his brain there may be the key that will unlock the whole case. In any event he may be useful in some small way.' The marshal picked up his hat and cane and rose to his feet. 'Now, Deputy, I am off to ask a few more questions.'

'Shall I watch your back, Marshal?'

'If you feel it necessary, but I am merely going to return to the Last Trading Post and probably remain there for the rest of the day. I have some work to attend to so I shall be in my room.'

'That's it, Marshal!' Murphy said wide-eyed. 'I forgot to tell yer. . . . She was shot over at the Last Trading Post.'

'I know . . . In fact, she was shot in my very room.'

'Now wait, Marshal,' Murphy said as he took to his feet. 'I ain't about to let that happen to you. I saw a chair in the corridor outside your room. I'm goin' to sleep in that.'

'Very well . . . if it pleases you.'

'It do,' Murphy replied.

CHAPTER 11

As the marshal and Murphy entered the reception of the Last Trading Post they saw Jason behind the desk, as usual, but sitting close by was a smartly-dressed man wearing a purple velvet collared smoking jacket, his salt-and-pepper-coloured hair standing out in contrast to his yellowing, rugged face.

He was enjoying a large cigar when Jason's face lit up with joy at the sight of Daniel. 'Lawrence,' he said as he clapped his hands together in excitement. 'This is the English marshal I told you about.' Then his expression dropped as if he had a bad smell under his nose. 'And this fellow with him is one of his deputies. And don't get too excited; the other one isn't much better either.'

Lawrence stood up, approached Daniel with a friendly smile and shook his hand vigorously. 'Pleased to meet you, Marshal. My partner has told me so much about you.'

Daniel gave a polite bow. 'I am not certain there is very much to know.'

118

'You are too modest,' Lawrence replied. 'You must dine with me tonight as my guest.'

'Thank you. I will look forward to it.'

'Shall we say . . . eight o'clock in the dining room?'

'Eight o'clock sharp, er . . Mister. . . ?'

'Rousseau.'

'French, I see.'

'On my father's side only, my mother was American.'

'Was?'

'Yes, they both passed away some years ago.'

'You have my condolences, Mister Rousseau. In life there is death.'

'And your parents, Marshal?'

'Thank you for asking, and I am most pleased to say they are both alive and well and living in Somerset.'

'Ah, Somerset, happy memories . . . When I was a young man I spent some time in England. Although I must admit I never reached Somerset, I travelled from London to York several times. My father was a businessman; he dealt in tobacco. I like to think he sold the finest cigars in the universe.'

'And I see you follow in his footsteps.'

'How very astute. How did you know?'

'Not astute at all, because from memory you have an outlet on the Strand in London and another in Goodramgate in York, and if I am not mistaken there is a third branch of Rousseau and Durand in an up-and-coming seaside resort on the west coast.'

'But how could you possibly know all that?'

119

'My father had a preference for one of your Coronas. In fact, the aroma tells me it is the very same type you are smoking.' He looked up as he wracked his brain. 'Les Dauphine de Versailles' if I remember correctly?'

'Very impressive, Marshal; I can see why you were asked to visit this humble little town.'

'I take it you moved out here for the good of your health?' Daniel asked.

'Now how did you know that?'

'Forgive me for mentioning it, but I could not fail to notice your complexion. If I am not mistaken you initially thought you were suffering from consumption, and thus moved out here for the benefits the dry atmosphere would offer. No doubt after spending some time here you realised that the change of air had little or no effect on relieving your symptoms, so you decided to get a second opinion and were consequently informed you had a respiratory problem that was not tuberculosis, but was more likely connected with the amount of cigars you smoke.'

Lawrence began a slow clap. 'Bravo, Marshal,' he said with admiration. 'I can see very little escapes your attention.'

'You are too kind, but perhaps you could just answer one tiny question?'

'Go ahead.'

'Miss Asquith. . . . She was shot in the very room I am using, correct?'

'Yes, correct, but everyone knows this.'

'Did she always use the same room?'

'Well, as a matter of fact, originally she had a room at the back but she complained so much about wanting to be able to see the main street I let her have my room, which, as I said, is the one you're in now.'

'And you have never moved back in?'

'No . . . I must admit I find the whole thing a little gruesome.'

'Do you know how many times she was shot?'

'Three . . . but why ask me?' he protested. 'The sheriff knows all about it.'

'But did you not hear the shots?'

'I didn't hear them because I was out of town on business, but Jason heard them as well as the other guests.'

'That's right, Marshal,' Jason interrupted. 'The first shots woke us all.'

'First shots?' Daniel asked. 'You mean there were more?'

'Yes, another five or six; they were fired by the killer as he rode away.'

'He and not she?'

'I was in the room next door to yours and I managed to get a glimpse of the killer as he rode away. That's when I saw him fire the other shots.'

'At whom was he shooting and with what?'

'He was just firing his pistol into the air,' Jason explained. 'He kept on shooting all the time he rode out of town.'

'And could you describe the man, or his horse? Anything?'

'Of course I can. I will never forget, because he looked dreadful with his black hat and red shirt over beige trousers. The whole thing clashed with his horse, which was a palomino.'

'From where did he fire the fatal shots?'

'From the balcony; he shot her through the open window.'

'Mister Rousseau, do you think there is a possibility the killer thought they were shooting at you?'

'That had crossed my mind, but who? I have no real enemies I can think of.'

'Of course not, forgive me for suggesting such a thing. It is a problem I have because I am a detective; I see danger everywhere.'

Murphy gave a grin of pride. 'When the marshal starts to askin' questions he always gets to the bottom of things. You know, I've seen him use special powder to tell him who's touched what and where. He calls 'em fingerprints, and he can do tricks and such. I tell yer, friend, he's one clever dude.'

Jason looked at Daniel, gave him a smile, clutched his arm and gave it a gentle squeeze. 'I can see that,' he said with a twinkle in his eye. 'He has my vote and that's for sure, although I must admit that hat and cane would simply have to go.'

The marshal gave a smile in return. 'You must forgive me,' he said. 'There is some urgent business we have to attend to, but I shall return later at eight.'

Murphy snarled at Jason as he turned to leave with Daniel. Outside he walked close to the marshal as they crossed the street, his face beaming like a cat that had got the cream. 'Marshal, I think I know who done it,' he said.

'Oh really, who?'

'That jaybird Jason,' he nodded. 'That's who.'

'My, my, Deputy; somehow I see you have hit the target.'

'Does that mean I'm right, Marshal?'

'Well, when I say you have hit the target, I mean you have done just that, but somehow you have avoided the bull's-eye in a manner that only you or Carver could achieve.'

'You mean I'm wrong?'

'Not entirely,' Daniel began. 'But tell me how you have come to your conclusion.'

'Well, it's easy, Marshal. That other dude, the smarmy one with the smarmy jacket, was out of town, which means the jaybird shot her.'

'And how, after he shot her, did he have the time to climb down from the balcony, reload his pistol, mount his horse and ride away without anyone else seeing him?'

Murphy rubbed his chin for a while then clicked his fingers. 'I got it,' he began. 'He shot her through the window, ran through the hotel, picked up another pistol, jumped onto his horse and rode away.'

'And I take it that after he had made enough noise to wake up everyone, he rode around for a while, doubled back unseen, changed his clothes and once again assumed his role as hotel manager?'

Murphy thought hard for a while. 'He could've done!'

Daniel gave a long sigh and stopped walking. 'Deputy,' he began. 'I take it you are somewhere in your late thirties or early forties?'

'Sure am, Marshal,' Murphy grinned inanely.

'And have somehow managed to arrive at this point in time in a reasonable condition?'

'I ain't with yer, Marshal.'

'No, indeed you are not, Deputy, so how can I phrase this in a manner more easily understandable to someone with limited intellect?' He thought for a second. 'I have it. If those grey cells that gamble and play between those ears of yours, those very same grey cells that drift randomly like the sand of the desert behind those eyes of yours, were to be collected, transformed into dynamite and ignited, the resulting explosion would not be enough to blow your hat off.'

Murphy fixed Daniel with a steely stare. 'Now listen, Marshal, there ain't no reason to go talkin' like that. I was only tryin' to help.'

'And your help in this matter has been invaluable, Deputy, and because you are taking such an interest in this case, I shall explain who did what and to whom, but the last piece of the jigsaw is missing: namely, why?' He leaned towards Murphy and lowered his voice. 'This is what happened: Jason, the jaybird, shot Miss Asquith with his own pistol and ran back to his room. Lawrence, the smarmy one, claimed to be out of town, but in reality was waiting on his horse until he heard the three shots, which gave him the signal to ride out of town making as much noise as possible, a noise so loud the entire population of Cactus Ridge could hardly fail to hear and assume the killer left, never to be seen or heard of again.'

'But that don't make no sense,' Murphy pointed out. 'If it were the smarmy one what did it, why would the other say what he was wearin'?'

'Do you really think I do not know what I am talking about? Think about it: there was a chance someone would have caught a glimpse of him as he rode away so to give a false description would have compromised the integrity of his story.'

'So why would he have not worn a disguise, or a mask?'

The marshal gave a small sigh. 'Of course he wore a disguise. Mister Rousseau does not wear cowboy clothes, but one thing he could not change is the colour of the horse he was riding.'

Murphy clicked his fingers. 'A palomino!'

'A palomino, indeed, and in their own private stables there are three horses: a chestnut, a bay and a palomino. Dick Turpin made a similar mistake insomuch as his horse was black, when he should have chosen a more common colour such as a bay.'

'Dick who?'

'Dick Turpin,' the astonished Marshal replied.

'I ain't never heard of him. Is he from the east?'

'You have never heard of Dick Turpin? Why, he was probably the most notorious of all highwaymen!'

'What did he do, Marshal?'

'What did he do? I should think that is quite

obvious: he held up stagecoaches at gunpoint, robbed the passengers and took any further monies that may have been in transit.'

'Where did he rob 'em?'

'In England, always somewhere between London and York.'

'And I guess you were the one that caught him, Marshal?'

'Of course I was not; he was hanged in 1739 for the murder of a keeper from Epping. I was not even born then.'

Murphy rubbed his chin. 'I still ain't never heard of him.'

'Do you know, Deputy, I find that most remarkable. His life story has been set to poetry; it has been in a host of penny dreadfuls . . . Whilst he was plying his trade his name was bandied about from John o' Groats to Land's End. Rewards were offered for his capture and after his death the press has continually made up reports of his so-called romantic lifestyle and his swashbuckling narrow escapes, and because of that they have managed to make him into some sort of folk hero, when in truth many of his escapades were either invention or falsely attributed to him.'

'The hell you say?'

'I do say, Deputy.' Daniel wagged his finger in frustration. 'Take his famous ride from Gadshill to York in fifteen hours. I will stake my reputation that was not done by Dick Turpin, but performed by another gentleman called Swift John Nevison some fifty years earlier.'

Murphy shook his head. 'You sure are a smart one, Marshal, but if'n you know they did it why don't we arrest 'em?'

'Proof, Deputy: we do not have any hard evidence by which we could prove they did it. All we have is conjecture and that is not sufficient to get a guilty verdict, but what we know already is probably enough to bring those two to justice. However, this will be confirmed when I receive a reply to a telegram I am about to send to a certain party in Chicago.'

'I ain't with yer, Marshal. You just said there ain't nothin' we can do and now you say we've done it.'

Daniel held his ears. 'Once again, a conversation with you makes my head hurt. I presume the term "ain't nothin' " is your method of saying "is not nothing", which is a double negative and thus has the reverse effect, when in actuality you intended to say "there is nothing".'

Murphy smiled. 'You sure do talk funny, Marshal.'

CHAPTER 12

'It's Custer!' Murphy screamed as he sat bolt upright and saw Carver's rugged face, grinning like a naughty schoolboy playing hookey. 'What the hell?' he blurted out as it became clear he had just been woken up by the sound of Moses' bugle.

'This 'ere bugle playin' is comin' on fine; just listen to this.' Carver screeched out a few twisted bars of something half resembling a tortured tune.

'What in tarnation do ya think yer doin'?' Murphy yelled.

'Gettin' ready for Sunday's precession; I'm gonna be right up in the front.' Carver said with pride.

'Now you lishen to this, Moses Carver: it ain't right you marchin' with all those ladies, you bein' a drinkin' man an' all. . . . It's just. . . . It's just. . . It ain't right, that's all.'

'I told ya, I ain't no drinkin' man no more.' He looked towards the heavens and gave a sigh. 'I have seen the light, brothers. I have seen the light.'

To Murphy's surprise, a gravel voice came from

under a pile of straw. 'Amen to that, brothers.'

Murphy cocked his head then grinned. 'Is that Old Casper?'

Carver nodded. 'Sure is. Sober as a judge. I reckon that stuff the marshal gave him has fixed him up a treat.'

Murphy threw one of his boots at the heap of straw. 'Hey, old-timer, let's have a good look at yer,' he laughed. 'Maybe we can get some sense out of yer.'

The mound of straw began to crumble and Casper fought his way out like a newly hatching chicken entering the world. He blew hard from his toothless mouth as he shook some straw from his head and pulled several blades from his beard. 'What he says is true. I ain't never goin' to touch another drop neither,' he said emphatically.

Murphy grinned. 'Why, you old ferret, you don't know what you're sayin'. You were on cactus juice . . . Sent you right crazy, it did. I'm talking about beer, whiskey and such, stuff that does yer good.'

Casper held his head in pain. 'I reckon I still ain't right yet, boys. What the heck happened to me?'

'We found ya in the sheriff's office. Do ya remember that?' Murphy asked.

'It's all a bit foggy, boys, but I reckon I can try.' His trembling fingers pointed at Murphy. 'Yes! There was another man . . . a marshal, I think.' Once again he held his head. 'A fire, there was a fire and I ran to getchya.' He began to smile. 'I knew I wasn't crazy.'

'Don't get too excited, old-timer,' Murphy pointed

out. 'There's a lot of things the marshal wants to ask yer, so best do some good thinkin' before he gets to see ya.'

'The marshal wants to see me?' he asked.

'He sure does. I reckon he wants to know why the townsfolk voted you to be their sheriff . . . I mean, you ain't exactly no spring chicken.'

Once again Casper clasped his hands on his head, shook it and took in a deep breath. 'I knew this town was rotten when they made me sheriff. That's why I sent a wire to the governor.'

'You?' Murphy gasped. 'You're the one who sent for us?'

'Not exactly . . . but maybe I did,' he slowly replied. 'I just wanted to let the governor know what was goin' on. I didn't think any more, I just sent him a wire for help . . . I don't really know why I did it. . . . Just did, I suppose.'

'That'll be a surprise for the marshal . . . Old Casper bein' the one who called us here.'

Carver laughed then gave several blasts on his bugle. 'That there tune means "get here quick". I reckon I could have called us here myself. 'Tain't no need for any telegraph when Moses Carver is around.'

'Will you stop blastin' that there trumpet? I ain't even got my boots on yet.'

Carver jumped up. 'I got practising to do, so I'll leave Casper with you. Tell the marshal I is following what he told me to do and stickin' close to Bathsheba.'

As he went down the loft ladder he gave out three more blasts. Murphy clenched his teeth in anger. 'Wait until you're outside before you commence to blastin' that there trumpet!' he shouted.

Carver laughed. 'My child,' he said softly. 'If you turn your back on Satan and his evil brew you'd be in a better disposition not to get quite so riled.'

'What in the name of hell are you jabberin' about?' Murphy shouted.

'That's what Bathsheba told me when I began cussin' because I stood in some horse shit.' As he left the livery stable and entered the street he started blowing hard.

Murphy turned to Casper, his face red with rage. 'And don't you say "amen to that, brothers" agen or I'll rip out your whiskers, make a cushion with 'em and stuff it down yer throat.'

Casper held up his hands in defeat. 'I wasn't planning on it, pilgrim . . . that's for sure.'

Murphy began to put on his boots as he threw Casper his bullwhip. 'Hey, old-timer,' he began. 'You any good with that?'

'I can hit a fly square between the eyes.'

'The hell you say?'

'The hell I do,' Casper said with pride, and then he thought hard, pulled his beard and sadly dropped his eyes. 'I suppose that was a long time ago now. Maybe I'm past it; maybe I'm a sad old man with nothing to offer anyone.'

Murphy smiled, reached across and put his hand gently on Casper's shoulder. 'You're never too old

131

when there's life in yer body . . . You're just a little rusty, that's all.'

Like a crumpled piece of paper, Casper slowly rose to his full height of four feet and a promise. 'I can remember the time when Black Jack Nelson called me out. You ever heard of him?'

Murphy shook his head. 'Don't reckon I have,' he replied.

'He was the meanest man this side of the Black Hills and everyone was in fear of him. Everyone, that is, except me.

'Well, one day Black Jack came to Beaver Skin to hold up the stage when it arrived.' Casper smiled, stared into the distance, shook his head clear and gave a cough. 'I knew it was Black Jack just as soon as I clapped eyes on him. He was a big fella: seven feet tall in his stocking feet and as broad as a barn, but it was his eyes what gave him away. One was brown and t'other steel blue, but together they were as cold as ice.

'Not many folk know this but Black Jack had a preference for a certain drink. Missouri Mousetrap it was called, and he couldn't never refuse a drop and once he started he'd go on until he could hardly walk. Well, I was standin' behind my counter when Black Jack came through the door. There were one or two other folk here and there but it was me he took to staring at. I remember trying hard not to blink for fear he'd think I was yella . . . My eyes burned but I kept on starin' right on back.

'Slowly he came my way and I noticed him getting

ready to pull both of his bone handled knives. Quick as you like I grabbed two bullwhips, came around and stood right in front of him. We looked at one another for maybe ten minutes before he went for his weapons, but in the time it takes a gopher to blink I cracked both whips and took his knives right from his hands. I cracked the one in my right hand, his britches belt cut in two and his pants fell to the floor. The one in my left took his hat clean off his head and sent it through the open window.

'I remember seeing that look on his face, that look of a beaten man, so I made him a Missouri Mousetrap on the house. He hightailed it after that and never came back.'

Murphy slapped his massive hands together and laughed. 'That's a good yarn, old-timer. I love a good yarn.'

' 'Tain't no yarn,' Casper protested. 'It happened in 1841, and folk still talk about it today nearly forty years later.'

'Whatever you say, Casper.'

'You called me Casper,' he said with surprise.

'That's your name, ain't it?'

'Sure is, but most folk call me old-timer or some such, but you just called me Casper.'

'Well, Casper,' Murphy smiled. 'Wait until you meet the marshal agen; he'll call you Mister Handyside no doubt.'

'That's right, I remember now. . . He does call me that,' Casper said with pride. 'Mister Handyside. . . . It does have a certain ring to it. Mister Handyside,

Mister Handyside, Mister Handyside.'

'What about Sheriff Handyside? Did anyone call ya that?'

'Let me think.' Casper looked up for inspiration. 'One fella did, as a matter of fact, the fella who runs the saloon, that fella with the fancy name . . . Roseau, I think?'

'He's slicker than a Mississippi boat rat, that's for sure,' Murphy replied. 'Whilst I think of it, who was it that gave you all the food and drink and such when you were hauled up in the jailhouse?'

'I used to sneak out after dark and find liquor and victuals hidden out back. I never seen who it was. Never wanted to neither.'

'So when this woman was shot, were you the sheriff at the time?'

'Sure was. I was made sheriff just a few days before she was shot.'

'Why in tarnation did you become sheriff? I mean, you could have said no.'

Casper pulled his grey beard through his hand once more and shook his head. 'When you get as old as me, young fella, you gets cold at night. Your bones begin to hurt from sleepin' in the livery, so the thought of a nice soft bed and somewhere to hang my hat was mighty appealing. At first I thought the townsfolk were serious and wanted me but now I know I'm just an old fool who should know better.' He sat back down slowly. 'I guess I'll just stay a bum and die a bum,' he said sadly.

'Come on now, Casper,' Murphy said kindly.

'Things ain't so bad . . . Look at me: I was all ready to go to jail for twenty years and along came these two twins and told me if I keep the marshal alive for two years I gets to be a free man, and I gets a chunk of money into the bargain.'

'That so?'

'That's so. It just goes to show you never know what's around the next bend. Just wait until you meet the marshal agen. He sure is smart; he'll think of something.'

CHAPTER 13

The Sunday parade was almost ready to begin when Murphy, Daniel and Casper came out of the Baptist Tabernacle. 'Woo-wee! Sure is a pretty sight, hey, Marshal?' Murphy said as his eyes got used to the full light of the day.

Daniel placed his fedora on his head. 'I see the full use of red, white and blue has been achieved and maximised. Such propaganda makes it look as if the president himself was in favour of prohibition, or better still, the whole nation.'

'There must be a hundred or more,' Murphy observed.

Daniel gave a sigh, 'From that remark I assume arithmetic has never been your strong point.'

'What'll you mean by that, Marshal?'

'Well, apart from your desire to completely transform the English language into something only a select group of guttersnipes would understand, it would appear you now have similar designs on standard mathematics, so that twelve becomes six and

136

two hundred becomes one.'

'Well, I ain't too good at cipherin' and such.'

'Well, that is quite obvious, but when you were riding the range and looking after cattle, how would you know if you had too many or too little without being able to count properly?'

Murphy gave a childish grin. 'That's easy, Marshal: I just counts up to ten.'

'So how would you know how many there were if there were more than ten?'

'Two lots of ten.'

'Am I to understand ten is the most you can count up to and from there you count groups of ten until you have ten groups?'

'I think I know what you mean, Marshal.'

'So what if there are fields full of cattle? What if the whole of Texas was covered in cattle? How would you count them then?'

'Couldn't, Marshal . . . but if'n there was as many as you say, nobody would miss a few now, would they?'

Disbelievingly, Daniel stared Murphy in the eyes. 'I really think you are serious,' he said.

Casper pointed excitedly. 'There's Carver!' he shouted. 'And just like he said, he's right up front.'

The spectacle of it all was breathtaking as the ladies took their positions and the drums began to beat. Banners held high they began to march slowly up the high street and towards the Ace in the Hole saloon. Carver had almost learned how to play 'Onward Christian Soldiers' and whenever he could he added the occasional note to the whole orchestration of the piece. Slowly and with solid determination, the line moved forward until one onlooker threw an egg, which narrowly missed Carver and hit Bathsheba square on the shoulder.

'Who threw that?' Moses shouted as he stopped in his tracks, only to see the scurrying shape of a cowboy disappear in between the milliners and the gunsmiths' store. 'You son of a bitch, I'll get ya,' he shouted as he pointed to his right, hitting a lady on the side of her head and removing her bonnet. 'Oh, beggin' your pardon, lady, that was an accident,' he jabbered as he bent down to pick up her hat, causing the lady behind him to trip and fall, which in turn happened to the next and the next. Soon the entire procession was a mixed pile of bodies scattered in different directions and positions, whilst the bass drummer at the rear continued to mark time and bang on regardless.

Murphy rocked with laughter. 'Hey, Carver,' he shouted. 'Can you play "The Walls Came A-Tumbling Down"?' But Carver was far too busy trying to grapple a rather stout lady to her feet, then innocently dusting her down and getting a good old-fashioned slap in the face for his trouble. 'Hey, brother Carver,' Murphy shouted again. 'Why don't ya turn the other cheek?'

Carver tripped up, fell backwards and crushed a trombone, causing a nearby cowboy to burst into fits of laughter. 'If'n that don't beat all,' he grumbled through gritted teeth as he threw a well-aimed punch at the laughing man.

The cowboy's two friends pounced on Carver, knocking him to the floor, so Murphy rushed to his aid. Soon pandemonium reigned and the whole street was a mass of brawling ladies, bandsmen, hooligans, drunkards and cowboys.

The marshal and Casper sat on some nearby stairs and watched as the fracas escalated. 'It would appear this sort of thing happens quite a lot in this country,' Daniel said casually.

'I reckon you're right, Marshal,' Casper agreed as he toyed with his bullwhip.

After a few minutes, high jinks gave way to frivolity, which in turn became anger and finally rage as a cowboy pulled a pistol on Carver. After a few moments everybody stood quiet and still. 'Will you two children behave?' the marshal snapped as he broke the silence.

The cowboy held up his spare hand as if pushing Daniel away. 'Stay out of this, Marshal, it's none of your business. This is between him and me and I'm goin' to blow his head off.'

Daniel gave a withering sigh. 'Why is it that everyone in this country is hell-bent on settling minor disagreements with the aid of some sort of firearm? And in this particular case, *you*, sir, are brandishing a pistol and *he* is not. Now that is hardly cricket.'

The cowboy looked quickly to one of his friends. 'Billy boy, throw him a pistol.'

His friend threw a gun to the floor in front of Carver. 'Go on now,' he growled. 'Pick it up.'

The marshal rolled his eyes. 'Oh, this is just what we wanted,' he said sarcastically. 'Another moron joining in on the farce.' He threw his hands up in despair. 'Very well, if this is how you people deal with slight differences of opinion, carry on by all means. Once again I shall remove myself from the field of battle and hope you both come to some sort of amicable decision, but if you do not I would rather be sat somewhere else.' He pointed to the cowboy. 'And you, young man, have not taken full stock of the situation, which is to say that, if by some strange quirk of fate you did manage to shoot my deputy, this other one on your left is equally eager to "blow your head off" and will obviously do so.'

'The marshal's right. Don't try it, Carver,' Murphy shouted. 'He's got the drop on ya.'

The cowboy began to grin a savage grin. 'I thought it was. . . . You're the great Moses Carver. . . . Well, you're not so great now. . . . You're yella.'

Carver's blood began to boil as he looked at the Colt lying before him.

'Go on, you coward, grab the gun or I'll shoot you where you stand.'

'Easy, Carver,' Murphy said calmly. 'He won't shoot.'

Carver's right hand began to move slightly downwards as the cowboy began to giggle hideously. 'He's gonna try it, boys. He's a dead man.'

Suddenly a whoosh and a crack sent the cowboy's gun to the floor as Murphy pulled his pistol. The third cowboy made a bid to pull his, but Murphy cocked his hammer and stopped him. 'I ain't gonna miss from here,' Murphy drawled.

Carver looked his adversary straight in the eyes and said, 'Now we're even, why don't you go for your gun now?'

The cowboy clenched his bloodstained right hand. 'That bullwhip has damn near cut my hand off,' he pleaded. 'I can't use it.'

'Then we'll both use the other one,' Carver growled as he held the back of his belt with his right hand.

The cowboy nervously rocked from side to side. 'Marshal,' he screamed. 'This ain't fair. If I go for my gun, this man will kill me for sure. That's murder, Marshal, murder in cold blood.'

Daniel let out a second audible tut. 'Now let me see . . . Ah, yes. From memory I was told to stay out of this. You also informed me it was none of my business and made it perfectly clear the whole incident is between the pair of you; but now things are not going the way you want them to, you have decided to ask for my help. Well, whilst I consider your request I shall leave you to placate my deputy before he "blows your head off", as you put it.'

Carver's eyes narrowed as he gritted his teeth. 'I'm getting impatient. Go for it, pilgrim.'

The cowboy dropped to his knees and held his hands high in the air. 'I'm sorry, I'm so sorry,' he shouted.

'Deputy,' the marshal interrupted. 'I must insist you do not shoot this man.' Next he looked at

Murphy. 'And that also goes for you. . . . Would you be so kind as to withdraw your pistol from the action?'

Carver's temper cooled down as Murphy holstered his gun but the cowboy saw his chance and went to grab his pistol. A swift kick in the face from one of Carver's size ten boots lifted him off his knees and sent him on his back, out cold. 'Some folk never learn,' he said as he shook his head.

'What shall we do with 'em, Marshal?' Murphy asked.

'Oh, nothing,' he replied as he looked at the other cowboys. 'Take him away and leave town.'

The other cowboys picked up their comrade. 'Are we banned from Cactus Ridge, Marshal?' one asked.

'Not at all. . . . You are hereby banished for a period of one or two days, which is roughly the time it will be necessary for us to remain in this town.'

'Thank you, Marshal, it won't happen agen,' they said.

Murphy came running up to Daniel. 'Did I hear ya right? We are goin' to leave soon? Does that mean you're goin' to arrest that pair of popinjays?'

'It does not, Deputy. You see, we have no real proof of their guilt.'

'But you know they did it, Marshal.'

'Indeed I do, but the instructions I have is to "bring the guilty parties to justice", and that is precisely what I have done.'

'I ain't with yer, Marshal.'

Daniel turned around and gave a sniff. 'Is that

wood smoke I can smell?'

'Yes,' Murphy pointed. 'It's comin' from the bake house.'

'Fire!' Carver shouted. 'Someone get some buckets and we'll see what we can do to beat out the flames.'

Daniel stood in disbelief. 'I am completely flabbergasted. Once again the pair of you have somehow managed to continue with your ludicrous desire to reduce the number of functional buildings in Cactus Ridge!'

'It ain't our fault this time, Marshal,' Murphy insisted.

'Ah-ha!' Daniel said knowingly. 'So you admit the other times were your fault.'

'Now that ain't fair, Marshal,' Murphy complained. 'We've done nothin' wrong.'

'Nothing wrong?' Daniel screeched. 'Do you realise the bakery staff have been working overtime to accommodate the town's temporary population increase? They have been busy since three o'clock this morning looking forward to this wonderful bonanza and you two have probably ruined everything by your street antics.'

'How is it to do with us, Marshal?'

'It is obvious, Deputy, because whilst you were prancing about like a pair of farceurs, the bakery staff were distracted, the results of which is this fire.'

'It's only a small one this time, though,' Murphy insisted. 'We'll soon put it out.'

Daniel gave a long sigh. 'Very well, Deputy; both

you and Carver render some assistance whilst Mister Handyside and I observe.'

Carver gave a grin. 'Hey, I almost forgot!' he exclaimed. 'Old Casper did real good. Well done, old-timer.'

Casper's chest swelled with self-respect.

CHAPTER 14

Murphy took to the driver's seat on Daniel's caravan, rang the bell and the pair of greys began to walk. 'You two ornery critters had better learn to do as I tell yer, and pretty soon,' he said out loud. 'Havin' to ring this goddamned bell just ain't right.'

He pulled up outside the Last Trading Post where Carver was waiting. 'Hey, Murphy,' he shouted. 'Ain't you trained these two yet? It looks mighty queer a grown man havin to ring a tinsy winsy little bell to get those critters to move.'

'Haw, haw, ain't you the smart one? Now listen to me, Moses Carver: I ain't the one who got drunk yesterday and let my darling Bathsheba find me sparkin' with Lolita from the cathouse.'

'Now that ain't fair and you know it. All I did was take a little sip to settle my nerves, that's all.'

'Judging by how big a sip you took, you must have been pretty nervous.'

Carver folded his arms and sulked.

'Oh come now, Carver,' Murphy said sympathetically. 'She weren't right for you . . . You're not a wimp, you're better'n that . . . What you need is a few days away from here and that little lady will be nothing more than a memory.'

Carver raised his head slowly and grinned. 'I got pretty good with the bugle though.'

'You ain't bringin' that with you, is ya?'

'Lost it! Or did I sell it? To tell you the truth, I ain't certain because I was too drunk.'

Murphy gave a laugh. 'Now that's the Moses Carver I know.'

The hotel door opened and Daniel appeared. 'Now if you two get my bags, we can be on our way back to Crows Creek in no time at all.'

Murphy jumped down. 'Just as you say, Marshal.'

'And do be careful: in some of those boxes there are very delicate pieces of scientific equipment.'

'Leave it to us, Marshal,' Carver said as Daniel saw Casper running towards them.

'Marshal!' he shouted as he ran. 'Marshal . . . I want to say thanks.'

Daniel waited until Casper came up close. 'My dear fellow, do my eyes deceive me? Is this the same man we encountered the first time we visited the sheriff's office? My word, you do look better.'

'Marshal, I feel like a new man.' He pointed to the sheriff's office. 'They're fixin' it up right now. I reckon I can move in next week. In the meantime, I'm stayin' with Klondike over at the saloon.'

Daniel patted Casper on the back. 'Well, Sheriff

Handyside,' he began. 'I'm certain these good people will show you a little more respect from now on, but remember what I have told you: "suspect no one, yet suspect everyone".'

Casper scratched his head. 'I ain't sure what you mean, but I'll bear it in mind, Marshal.'

Murphy and Carver reappeared with some luggage. 'Hey, Casper,' Murphy said with a smile. 'Are you wearin' that sheriff's badge agen?'

'Sure am. The marshal said I was still the sheriff.'

Carver looked at Daniel. 'That true, Marshal?'

'Of course it is . . . Mister Handyside, or should I say Sheriff Handyside, will make a very fine sheriff. Besides, it is what these good town's folk wanted so it is what they are going to get.' He placed his fedora on his head. 'Cactus Ridge has a very fine justice system in the form of Sheriff Handyside with James Wanamaker as deputy; therefore I do not see any reason why we cannot allow the situation to continue.'

After all of the marshal's luggage had been stored, Murphy gave the bell a ring and they turned to return to Crows Creek. A few miles down the trail, Murphy became curious. 'Marshal?' he asked 'I ain't sure what went on there. I mean, you know who shot that woman and you did nothin' about it.'

Daniel came from the rear and sat next to Murphy. 'On the contrary, Deputy, we achieved our goal, and a little more.'

'But those killers are free.'

'Indeed they are, but perhaps I should explain.

The lady who was murdered was not quite who she appeared to be, and our part in this grizzly affair is simply to inform a government official in Chicago who perpetrated the crime.'

'You mean she wasn't part of that women's army but a government spy?'

'You mean the Temperance League, and that is not what I was going to say. The file I was given by the twins explained who she was and where she came from. What it did not explain is why she was murdered and by whom.'

'But you got it figured out, I guess?'

'Indeed I have. You see, the lady in question was orphaned by the age of six; she grew up on the streets of Chicago along with some other poor unfortunate children. She grew up tough and streetwise, and soon chance would have her meet a gentleman whose name I cannot divulge, but it is safe to say he has considerable influence in the Mafia of America, not to mention the government. He employed her to help run some of his various businesses in and around Chicago.

'Now this gentleman – we shall call him Mister Big – took quite a shine to Miss Asquith and wanted her as his mistress, but that was never going to happen because – unbeknown to him – she had turned to God, so she left his employ with his blessing and a small annual increment that enabled her to join the temperance movement and tour America. Now when she came to Cactus Ridge, fate dealt a hand she never imagined would happen when she recognised

Jason Monkshood, because at one point in his life he too worked for Mister Big and, rather stupidly, cheated him out of a large sum of money. Jason ran away to Europe, where he met Lawrence Rousseau, and together they set up a business partnership such as they have today.

'Miss Asquith found herself torn between God and her loyalty to Mister Big, but her loyalty won over and she sent a telegram to Mister Big informing him where Jason could be found. Unfortunately, Jason was unaware she had done this and because he could not afford Mister Big knowing his whereabouts, he took the chance to silence her for good. I expect the pair rather thought that hatred for the temperance movement and their leaders would cloud the motive for her death.'

Murphy placed a cheroot in the side of his mouth. 'One thing I don't get, Marshal: what about Casper? I mean, he ain't no sheriff so why did the townsfolk choose him?'

'There was nothing strange about the appointment of Sheriff Handyside, because the townsfolk rather ran the town themselves with the help of the deputy, James Wanamaker, and they did a very good job of it. Mister Handyside was employed as a token sheriff; it suited him and them at the same time.'

Murphy lit his smoke and took a deep draw. 'Well, why give him all that cactus juice, and what was all that blather about Billy the Kid?'

'The murderers could not risk the sheriff investigating just in case he found out the truth, so they drugged him and, using the drainage system of the building opposite the jail, they spoke to him and planted the scare in his brain about Billy the Kid. After all, Mister Bonny has supposedly shot three officers of the law, so to the mind of someone under the influence of peyote the threat would appear very real indeed. As for the deputy . . . Well, he also liked the system the way it was and did not want anyone coming to town and 'making waves', as it were. However, he did not and could not know how fond Mister Big was of Miss Asquith, nor could he know about Jason Monkshood's past. If he had he would probably have notified Mister Big himself.'

Murphy looked puzzled. 'So what'll happen to those two popinjays who own the Last Trading Post?'

'Well, Deputy, according to my calculations they will guess why we have left Cactus Ridge and will make themselves rather scarce as quickly as possible, probably selling their hotel to James Wanamaker, the proprietor of the Ace in the Hole Saloon, who could easily afford it.'

'Do ya reckon old Casper will manage to cope as a sheriff? I sure don't want the old-timer to get himself shot; maybe we should have stayed a few more days to see how he was gettin' on.'

'Are you serious, Deputy? You are talking about the man who ended the career of Black Jack Nelson.'

Murphy laughed. 'He told ya that yarn too?'

'No yarn, Deputy, it really did happen. It was well documented and in the report given to me by the government twins.'

150

'The hell ya say?'

'There you go with that expression. Sometimes it can be very tiresome.'

'The hell ya say?' Suddenly Murphy's eyes grew wide with excitement. 'Hey, Marshal, you're wrong about who asked us to come to Cactus Ridge because it was Old Casper who wrote to the governor.'

'Sheer coincidence, that is all.'

CHAPTER 15

The thought of getting back to Crows Creek made the journey seem long and hard, and after five days Murphy was getting impatient to be back in the comfort of his bed. 'I wish this caravan could go a little quicker, Marshal. It ain't hardly Wells Fargo.'

'Patience, Deputy,' Daniel replied. 'Crows Creek is not going anywhere.'

A few hot, dry hours passed by until Carver rode up close. 'Hey, Murphy, have you seen what I think I've seen?' he whispered.

'Yep.'

'How many do ya think?'

'Judging by the dust cloud . . . more than ten.'

'Maybe it's Geronimo agen?' Carver suggested.

'Maybe.'

'They've been tailin' us for a while.'

'I reckon you're right,' Murphy agreed.

'Should we speed up?' Carver asked.

' 'Tain't no point: this damn blasted caravan ain't built for speed. Besides, the marshal thinks more about his stupid bottles than he does of us. Best we just keep on movin' and set up camp when we get to those hills o'er yon.'

Slowly they trundled on, through rocky country and chaparral until they came close to a bend in the trail to the right of a steep stone outcrop. 'Hey, Murphy,' Carver said through gritted teeth, 'this comin' up is a good place for an ambush; keep your eyes peeled.'

As they turned the corner, they were greeted by eighteen mounted, heavily armed Mexicans, with what appeared to be their leader out front. '*Buenos días*, gentlemen,' he said with an evil smile. 'My, it is hot. . . . Not a good day to be travelling, no?'

He removed his sombrero, wiped his brow, slapped it back on his head and grinned. 'My men are curious. As for me, I am not, but you see they wish to know what you have in the little fancy wagon.'

'Nothin',' Murphy replied.

The leader wagged his finger. 'Tut, tut, tut. I ask you as a friend and you refuse to tell me.' He turned his head to look at his men and turned back again. 'My men have many guns but they do not point them.' He wagged his finger again. 'I think you are very rude, so I ask again: what do you have in the fancy wagon?'

'Me,' the marshal replied as he came to sit next to Murphy. 'And may I enquire as to your business?'

'English!' he beamed. 'I like the English very much.' He leaned forwards in his saddle and rested both hands in its pommel. 'Perhaps you will save me the trouble of looking, my friend, and tell me what is in your fancy wagon?'

'My personal belongings: science equipment and medicines, mostly,' Daniel replied.

'I will buy them,' the leader said as he ordered two of his men to take a look. 'I will also make your journey a little easier by buying from you your weapons and horses. A stroll through the desert will do you all good.'

'This is an outrage!' Daniel snapped. 'Wait until your president hears about this.'

His men began to laugh. 'My friend, I see you have *cojones*. That is good in a man, but out here, and when you are so helpless, it does little good. But, I tell you what I will do. I am a reasonable man, so I will give you two pesos for everything you have.'

'You, sir, are a bully.'

'Now I am hurt, my friend, so now I will only pay you one peso.'

Without warning, two of his men fell off their horses as two arrows found their mark, then three more hit their targets, followed by another three. '*¡Vamos!*' he shouted as he pulled hard on the reins to turn his horse. '*Andale amigos.*'

An Indian war cry could be heard to be getting louder as the ground shook from the pounding of horses' hoofs. Soon the Mexicans were on the run followed by Geronimo's warriors, screaming as they fired arrows, rifles and pistols – all except for one, who stopped and jumped to the ground. 'So we meet again, Marshal. Your God is kind to you.'

154

'Soaring Hawk, it is good to see you,' Daniel said as he shook the brave's hand.

'I must go,' the Indian said as he vaulted back on his horse. 'We have spent many weeks searching for those men. Once we kill them we shall go home.' Then he gave out a bloodcurdling cry and sped off in pursuit.

After the dust had died down Murphy gave a relieved sigh. 'I reckon we'd better be makin' tracks, Marshal.'

'I think you are perfectly right, Deputy.'

After two more weary days on the trail, Crows Creek finally came into sight and Carver rode up next to Murphy. 'Stop this here wagon and let me get on,' he said.

Murphy did as he was asked. Carver tied his horse next to Sea Biscuit and jumped up next to Murphy. 'Do you know something, Carver? What with Geronimo and those Mexicans, I reckon the marshal has some sort of guardian angel.'

Carver thought, and then rolled a cigarette. 'I reckon you're right, but there were these three dudes I once met in Wichita and they had this dancing bear. Talk about lucky.'

Murphy's eye grew wide as he grabbed Carver's arm. 'Wichita? I told ya about that there tall woman I met there, remember?'

'I sure do, my friend: tall and slim with a lock of red hair. Anyway, as I was telling yer . . . They said they'd been all across the country with this bear, sayin' as how it could beat anyone at blackjack. Well, at the time there was a new marshal named Mike Meagher and he had a deputy called Wyatt Earp. Meanest son of a bitch I ever did see: he'd done just about everythin' from horse thievin' to buffalo huntin', but most of all he was good with a gun. Not fast, you understand, but cool and deliberate, and he'd shot many a man who tried to cheat him at cards; some folk say as many as fifteen had been put into the ground by Earp.'

'Now hold it there,' Murphy interrupted. 'I heard of Wyatt Earp. He dealt faro at the Long Branch saloon and trailed Dave Rudabaugh right down from Santa Fe to Fort Clark, but I ain't never heard he'd shot fifteen men.'

Carver's face lit up with a boyish grin, then he pointed his finger and gave Murphy a friendly poke. 'Well, you don't hear nothin' and you don't count too good either, so what I'm telling yer is right.'

Murphy rubbed his chin in thought and shook his head. 'Well, I don't know if'n what you're sayin' is right, that's all.'

Carver frowned and turned to face Murphy, 'Do ya want me to tell yer or not?'

'I expect so,' Murphy answered.

'Then I shall continue. Anyway, him and his brother owned a saloon and brothel in Wichita, and these three dudes with their bear thought it a good idea to show off their critter and win a few dollars, so they went and told him all about their clever animal and how it could play blackjack.'

156

Murphy gasped, 'The hell ya say? A real bear what could play blackjack?'

Carver gave a knowing nod. 'The hell I do say . . . Anyway, Earp got real excited and could see the bear was a gold mine, so made a big thing about it. He spread the word and told everyone in town to be there on Saturday night. Well, other folk soon got to hear, and this particular Saturday night people of all descriptions came to see this card playin' bear. There were cowboys, engineers, drifters, ranchers, farmers and gamblers, so many folk they all couldn't fit in the bar. Now, Earp was one hell of a card player himself and he took to playin' this 'ere bear himself. The way it worked was each of these dudes would take turns in showin' the bear its cards and if'n the bear took a good look and gave a nod of its head, the bear would be askin' for a third card or even a forth.'

Murphy leaned back and pushed his hat high on his forehead. 'Now you're pullin' my craw even more 'n ya were when ya started.'

'I ain't never . . . I swear I is telling the truth.' He opened his eyes wide, licked his finger and crossed his heart. 'This 'ere bear wore a pair of red short bitches, a black-and-white shirt and sat on its backside whilst drinkin' beer from a bottle it held itself.'

'The hell ya say?'

'The hell I do. Anyway, as the night went on this bear kept on a-winnin' an' winnin' until it had won all Earp's money. It damn near cleaned four more dudes out as well. I tell ya, Murphy, I ain't never seen anything like it afore. Anyway, it came to closing and these dudes and their bear had won over a hundred dollars and Earp was real mad. As they were gatherin' all their dollars, Earp came up and asked for one last game.'

'The hell ya say?'

'The hell I do. . . . He took some money from his cash box, slapped it down on the table and pointed to three other dudes sayin' as how they were to hold the cards and not the bear's owners. I swear, Murphy, I have never seen a saloon so quiet as the cards were dealt. First one card each, then a second. Next one of the dudes that Earp had ordered to help showed the bear its hand and it did nothin'. Earp told the next dude to show the bear its cards, and still it did nothin' on account of it was the bear's owners who told it what to do by gently tappin' the bear on its toes when it was time to twist or fold.

'Earp must have figured this and stood up, sayin' as to how he could smell a rat and he was goin' to skin those three dudes alive when he caught 'em, but the bear's owners had slipped out when everyone was watchin' the card game. Earp's face went bright purple as he pulled his pistol and ran after those men. He knew they hadn't left town because of their bear, so all he had to do was lock up the bear until they surfaced, but Earp was in no mood to wait so he almost tore the town apart searchin'.'

Carver went silent to build up the tension as Murphy listened intensely. 'Well? Did he find 'em?' he asked.

Carver nodded his head. 'Sure did. He found 'em

158

skulkin' about behind a great big mountain of horse manure. Boy, were they in trouble!'

Murphy screwed up his face in confusion. 'I thought you said this was a story about good luck?'

'It is if'n you let me finish. Next, Earp strode up with a Colt in one hand and a Derringer in the other and was in the mood to send 'em to kingdom come, when all of a sudden he burst out laughin'. Half the saloon had followed him and they all commenced to laughin' as well.'

Murphy looked at Carver in disbelief. 'You mean to say he let 'em go?'

Moses shook his head. 'Not exactly; he took all the money he'd lost and some more, sold the bear and ran 'em outta town.'

Murphy looked puzzled. 'Carver, have you been drinkin' that cactus juice old Casper took to drinkin'? You said this was a yarn about good luck.'

'I know I did, and it is. . . . You see, the bear got bought by this rancher . . . he had a soft spot for bears and he let it live peacefully on his range with all the other bears he'd bought.'

Murphy slapped his thigh amid bursts of laughter. 'That sure is a hell of a tale,' he said as he turned to share the story with Daniel. 'Did ya hear that, Marshal? It was the bear that was lucky.'

'May the saints preserve us,' the marshal mumbled as they trundled slowly towards Crows Creek.

'Just comin' into town, Marshal,' Murphy shouted. 'Can't say as I can see anyone around; it's like a ghost town.'

Daniel came forward and looked out across the deserted street.

'Hello!' Carver shouted. 'Is anyone there?'

From the sheriff's office, a nervously excited Clarence and Claude came scurrying towards them. 'We are glad to see you, boys!' Clarence said.

'Indeed we are,' Claude agreed.

'The Bannisters have been broken out of jail by Stitch Logan and his gang.'